A
GIFT
FOR
A
GIFT

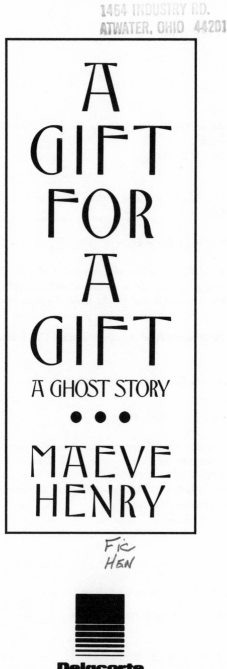

A GIFT FOR A GIFT

A GHOST STORY

• • •

MAEVE HENRY

Delacorte Press

Published by
Delacorte Press
Bantam Doubleday Dell Publishing Group, Inc.
666 Fifth Avenue
New York, New York 10103

This work was originally published in Great Britain in 1990 by William
Heinemann Ltd.

Library of Congress Cataloging-in-Publication Data

Henry, Maeve.
    A gift for a gift / Maeve Henry.
        p.   cm.
    Summary: Fran, a British teenager from a troubled home, meets a
mysterious man who holds the power to fulfill all of her wishes.
    ISBN 0-385-30562-1
    [1. Wishes—Fiction.   2. Magic—Fiction.   3. Family problems—Fiction.
4. England—Fiction.]   I. Title.
PZ7.H39397Gi   1992
[Fic]—dc20   91-16294
                                                                   CIP
                                                                    AC

Interior design by Diane Stevenson/Snap •Haus Graphics

Manufactured in the United States of America

May 1992

10   9   8   7   6   5   4   3   2   1

BVG

FOR
JOHN

• • •

CHAPTER ONE

FRAN KELLY STOOD OUTSIDE the park at three in the morning, crying a little and pretending, though there was no one to see, that she wasn't. She was a thin small-featured girl of fifteen, dressed in a baggy gray sweater and short black skirt. Her face, always pale, was so white that the freckles normally invisible in winter showed up clearly. She had been walking around town all night, too stubborn to go home.

It had been just once too often. When she came downstairs at ten o'clock to find the boys still watching television with all that mess untouched, she yelled that she'd had enough, she was leaving, and ran out of the house without even a coat. The bus into town was just pulling away from the stop; she had caught up with it, waving her hands like mad at the driver, who saw her and opened the doors. She jumped aboard and took her seat feeling reckless and extravagant. When they swayed into the High Street, she got out. The gang from the development was hanging around outside Mc-

Donald's, blocking the sidewalk and forcing people into the path of the cars. Fran kept to the other side of the street. She began to walk slowly along, looking into the store windows and telling herself what she would buy if she had the money. Rage gave her a glow almost like happiness. She passed a pub doorway and stopped to inhale the warm heavy smell and listen to the thick noise of male voices, but she didn't go in. She reached the movie theater and watched the crowd come out, faces flinching in the cold air and the streetlights. Everything around her seemed to have the vivid strangeness of a foreign place. She walked and watched and felt intensely alive.

At last the pubs closed and the streets began to empty and Fran joined the line for the last bus home. She leaned against the corner of the shelter, listening to the bickering couples and feeling the wind sweep in through the broken glass. Her rage was flat and cold now, but still stubborn. She didn't realize how stubborn until the bus swung into sight. As everyone pushed forward to get on, Fran stood back and let them pass. When all the fares had been paid and the last passenger had moved down to find a seat, the driver looked across at Fran inquiringly. She said nothing, and met his glance with a hard stare.

"Up yours, then," he said, and closed the doors.

The bus eased away, stirring the litter at Fran's feet. It gave her an odd empty feeling to see it go. For a moment she wondered if she should walk home. She looked at the clock in the jeweler's opposite. Eleven-thirty. The boys would still be up, dozing in front of the television with the jumble of dirty plates and toys around them. The muscles in her neck tightened. She couldn't go back to that. She couldn't. She forced herself to laugh and set off at a run down a side street. Let them find her missing in the morning!

By three o'clock she had stopped thinking about anything but how to make time pass. She was standing outside the locked park, waiting to find the energy to move on. Among the bushes, black under the streetlights, was a bird that rustled and sang. It seemed the only other living thing awake. Fran leaned against the park gates, hungry and cold and desperately tired, listening to that bird. When it stopped, she turned her head and watched the traffic lights changing at the end of the street. The street was empty and the lights went on changing and nothing living was there. The world was empty and nothing would ever change.

"But it has to," Fran said aloud. "There's got to be something, or I can't go on. I can't." She lifted her head and shouted:

"Where *are* you?"

In the silence, somewhere out of sight, a car started up and drove off. Then nothing. There was no answer. The world threatened to dissolve and Fran with it. She turned in a panic and ran, the only sound the scratch of her own shoes on the street; ran to the railroad bridge from which she could see the hospital and the station, places where people might be awake and at work. She grasped the metal paling and felt it shudder as a freight train passed underneath. It was then she started to cry. She was so tired.

She must have fallen asleep on her feet, for she came to herself with a start. Her body was a cold dead weight in which only her eyes were working. They focused on a sky that was gray and wet. Her clothes were wet and her hands still curved, white and bloodless, around the paling of the bridge. With a groan, Fran moved her feet. The pain of returning blood was intense. When the worst of it was over, her mind focused, animallike, on shelter. She had to get out of the rain.

She began to move slowly down the bridge toward the nearest houses. They formed a terrace looking over a small cricket field, all large and shabby, built of yellowish brick. Fran found herself walking past the first houses; she was drawn to one in the middle of the row by an attraction as strong as it was inexplicable. She opened the peeling gate and followed a path along the side of the house to the back. It was damp and mossy and led to what had once been a garden. There were steps leading up to French windows and down to a basement door. Fran crept down to the basement door and tried it, but it was locked. She tried the French windows. The handle turned in her hand, and she stepped inside.

The first thing she saw was an eye. Small and black and intelligent, it regarded her with an expression of delicate outrage. Too stunned by exhaustion to scream, Fran stepped back against the curtains and their movement brought more light into the room. It was a bird eyeing her, a long-legged bird with a sleek head and a curving beak. Fran did not move. Neither did the bird. Gradually she realized that it couldn't. It wasn't alive, it was stuffed. She opened the curtains a little farther and saw that the room was full of birds, brooding on nests or with wings stretched in flight; in glass cabinets or perched on the shabby furniture. To Fran all that mattered for the moment was that they were not going to raise the alarm. She stepped in among the birds, lay down on a sofa, and was asleep in less than a minute.

She woke feeling hot and heavy. She sat up quickly and found herself entangled in blankets. Her foot nudged something that fell off the sofa with a rubbery thud. Fran was up in a hurry, feeling for her shoes under the sofa. She wondered if you could be raped in your sleep and not know afterward. You've done some stupid things, she told herself, but this—
    "Don't go yet."
    It was a man's voice, light and pleasant.
    Fran stood very still.
    "Coffee first, and a hot bath, if you like. Anyone who can sleep in here deserves that much."

Fran forced herself to turn around. He didn't look like a maniac. (So what does a maniac look like, her brain demanded scornfully.) He was about thirty, not very tall, with a reddish beard and brown hair that was too long at the back. His skin was rather white, the sort of skin that never took a tan, however hot the summer. There were pouches under his eyes and he was a bit overweight. His clothes were like a teacher's, dark and rather shabbily formal—black shirt, black cords, gray tie. He was watching her as warily as she was watching him and he was standing between her and the French windows.

"I don't believe in luck," he said. "Otherwise I'd tell you you were lucky you chose this house. You'd have gotten more than blankets and a hot-water bottle in other places I can think of."

"I was tired," Fran said aggressively.

"So I saw."

She waited for him to say something else, but he didn't.

"You shouldn't leave doors open if you don't want people to come in," she said.

"You shouldn't, should you?" he agreed. "However you're here now, and you had some reason for coming, even if it was only to get a few hours' sleep, and it offends my notion of hospitality that you should leave looking like that. There's a mirror over the fireplace." Stung, Fran went to look at herself. She wished she hadn't.

"The bathroom's upstairs, first left. Milk and sugar in your coffee?"

"I have to go home," Fran said, looking past him toward the windows.

"There's a lock on the bathroom door." He was laughing at her. "The door's solid too. Even if I could find my ax, you'd have time to get out onto the roof."

"I have to go." Fixing him with a stare, she began to move toward the windows.

"If you must." He hesitated, then added, "Fran."

She stopped dead. "How did you know my name? I don't know who you are."

He smiled. "My name's Michael. Come back when you're less scared."

"I'm not scared of you," Fran lied.

"Then you've been very badly brought up. But I expect I'll be able to judge that from the state of the bathroom, won't I?"

I can always get out onto the roof, Fran thought as she climbed the stairs. But there was no immediate danger. Michael had gone down the hall into the kitchen where she could hear him opening cupboards. When she reached the landing she turned around to look. As she did so her feeling of attraction, almost of recognition, returned with great strength. But it was an odd house. The wallpaper in the hall had faded to buff color, faintly striped, and there were two dark oil paintings of dead birds and fruit hanging on the far wall. On the landing there was a big bookcase, stuffed with everything from paperbacks to leatherbound tomes. Fran itched to pull a few things out and look at them, but she was afraid Michael would catch her at it. The house did not fit Michael, she realized suddenly. It had the feeling of someone old, someone you could trust.

•

When she saw the bathroom she was glad she had put off going home. It was ridiculously large and old-fashioned–looking. The tub was enameled iron, narrow and deep, like a coffin with white clawed feet. There were blue and white windmill tiles on the walls, and the floorboards were thickly varnished. Beside the bath there was a towel rack with six spotless white towels on it. There was nothing else in the room, not even a sink. All that space cried out for action. While the water was drumming into the tub, Fran stripped off everything but her socks and began to slide along the slippery boards, lurching from one corner of the room to another, arms spread wide as she banged into the walls, giggling like an idiot.

When she'd had enough, she turned off the taps, took off her socks, stepped gingerly in and lay back amid the steam. It was glorious. At home the tub was so dirty she never bothered. She closed her eyes and moved her legs gently to feel the water over them. All that was lacking was something to read.

"Coffee!" Michael thumped on the door.

Fran's head jerked up. She listened to the retreating footsteps, then hauled herself out of the water and into a towel. When she opened the door she saw a tray. Not just coffee, breakfast: a Danish pastry, a package of salt and vinegar chips, and a juicy peach. Fran grinned. It was exactly what she would have chosen.

•

A GIFT FOR A GIFT

When the water was gray and scummy, cooling fast, Fran reluctantly got out. She wrapped herself in the biggest of the towels and sat down cross-legged on the floor. Idly she wrote her full name in steam across the boards. *Francesca Deirdre Kelly.* It always appalled her to see it, especially that Deirdre. As she got dressed she was careful to blot out the name with her shifting feet. When she was ready she ran her fingers through her short damp hair and made a face. Now what?

Michael was sitting in the room with the birds, a book in his hand.

"Much better," he said as she came in. "Sit down, if you like. Though if you run away now, at least you won't disgrace me."

Fran went over to the chair opposite him, but couldn't quite bring herself to sit down.

"What are you reading?" she asked.

"Milton. *Paradise Lost.* Ever read it?"

Fran shook her head.

"But you like reading poetry."

Fran froze.

"You don't know that," she said.

"It's unusual to like reading and not school."

Fran's nails were cutting into the palms of her hands. "You can't know that," she said. "No one knows."

Michael laughed. "*You* know," he said. "And I guessed, like I guessed your name. It's a sort of trick. If I'm interested in someone and I concentrate, I can often learn things about them."

Fran was still scared. A magpie was perched on the table next to her. She stroked its stiff back for comfort, but when she took her hand away it smelled musty and unpleasant.

"I'm going home," she decided.

"But you don't want to go home."

Fran looked at him. He was watching her, his brown eyes friendly and amused.

"So you reckon you're a mindreader, do you?" she said with as much sarcasm as she could muster.

"Oh, if it's tricks you want," he said, "I can do any number."

Suddenly all the birds in the room were alive, beating at the walls of their glass cases or flying free. Fran covered her head to protect it from the frantic wings and dreadful noise.

"Stop it!" she shouted. "Michael, stop it!"

In an instant there was quiet. She looked at him.

"A trick," he said.

She turned her back on him. She was shaking.

"Fran," he said. She could hear him leaving his chair, coming toward her. "Not a trick, a mistake. I was hoping to interest you so much you'd want to come back."

His hand was on her arm. Fran pulled herself free. "I'm going," she said. "I have to go."

She was still afraid to look in his direction. So it would not feel too much like a retreat, she made a wide circuit of the room, pausing at a collection of photographs arranged on the piano. One of them, the picture of a woman in a hat frowning into the camera, caught her attention. She liked that face.

"Who is it?" she asked, turning the photograph to show Michael.

"The owner of the house."

"It isn't your house?" This time she looked at him. He smiled, and said: "You shouldn't leave doors open if you don't want people to come in."

CHAPTER TWO

IT WAS NO LONGER raining when Fran left the house, but brown water stood in the potholes and the railings of the cricket field were beaded with wet. Someone was having a piano lesson in one of the houses down the street. As Fran walked slowly past she felt cold and miserable. She was try-ing to avoid thinking about Michael.

At the corner she stopped an old man with a dog and asked him the time. When she learned it was after two she began to run. As she ran she became more and more panicky. Anything could have happened at home. Anything. Police, fire engines, and ambulances jostled against each other in her mind. But the general fear was deeper and harder to bear. She just shouldn't have left them. She must have been goddamn crazy. The words fell into a rhythm with her running. Goddamn crazy, goddamn crazy. She didn't think of catching a bus till she was halfway home and then she couldn't wait at the stop but had to keep moving. *Goddamn* crazy, *goddamn* crazy. She reached the turning into the passageway with a stitch in her side and no breath left.

There were no police cars. The road was empty except for two teenage girls leaning on strollers and sharing a cigarette. They watched Fran slow into a walk. One nudged the other and said something, and they both burst into raucous laughter as she passed. Fran knew the joke. She turned and gave them a stare full of hatred.

"Your bastard kids smell worse than I do," she yelled.

Screaming abuse followed her around the curve of the street, but they didn't come after her. She could see her mother's house now. Like all the others it looked as if it had been built back to front. The windows were small and set in odd places and the front door was narrow and unimpressive. Under the ground-floor window the trim was scratched and peeling and there was trash in the strip of grass beside the door. The curtains were still drawn and standing in the front-bedroom window was a half-full bottle of milk. It had been there so long Fran had stopped noticing it.

"I'm back," she shouted as she entered the house. No one replied. She laid her hand on the banister to go upstairs, then changed her mind and pushed her way through the cramped hallway, stumbling over the vacuum cleaner and the torn garbage bag that should have been put out yesterday. She went into the kitchen, which was small and filthy, slid a mug out of the heap in the sink, rinsed it under the cold tap, and drank. I needn't have worried, she thought sourly. No one else has.

As she went into the hall again she heard the muted sound of the television in the living room. Someone was home. She pushed open the door and saw Nigel sitting inches away from the screen, one hand in a box of cornflakes, staring and chewing openmouthed.

"So why aren't you at school?" Fran demanded.

"Franny!" Nigel leapt up, scattering cornflakes, and charged.

Fran took the familiar thud of him against her knees, then swung him up and carried him over to the settee, tipping him onto it. He was giggling as he landed, but his eyes were shining and there were the dirty marks of tears on his face.

"Come off it," Fran said almost angrily. "You knew I'd come back."

"Lee said you wouldn't. Lee said you'd gone off with someone."

"As if I would." Fran poked him in the stomach. The thought of Michael came back and she added: "As if anyone would have me, either."

The plates that had started last night's quarrel were still on the floor along with the rest of the mess. It seemed a long time ago now.

"Lee just went off to school, did he? He wasn't worried or anything?"

Nigel didn't know. "He just went."

"Goddamn him, then."

A GIFT FOR A GIFT

•

The room did smell bad, though. Fran went over to the window and wrenched it open. Outside was the tiny back garden: a shopping cart rusting on its side in the long grass, forgotten lengths of wood, and a sagging clothesline. But the cold fresh air made her want to clear everything up, never mind whose turn it was.

"Tea first," she said aloud. "I'll put the kettle on." Without turning around she added: "And I'm sorry you were scared."

When Nigel didn't say anything she went back to the settee and stooped over him. He was like their dad, fair and small-boned, delicate-looking. She pushed back the hair from his forehead and he stared up at her without smiling. Then he grabbed her hands and pulled.

"Don't do it again, Franny," he said. "Just don't."

"I won't," she said. "Promise."

When he let her go, she straightened up.

"Will you take some tea upstairs to Mom if I make it?"

Nigel shook his head.

"Lazy bastard." She aimed a punch that stopped just short of his ear.

"I wish you were our mom," Nigel said.

The bedroom light was off. Fran opened the door as quietly as she could. "You awake, Mom?"

She balanced the mug on a corner of the dressing table while she felt for the light switch. The smell of the room was so bad she had to breathe through her mouth.

Her mother sat up with a jerk as the light came on. "What time is it?" she demanded with a huge yawn.

"Three-something. I thought you'd like a cup of tea."

Fran fiddled with the bottles of pills on the bedside table while her mother blew on the tea to cool it. It embarrassed her to see her mother in a nightgown. She was so big and sloppy-looking. When she was dressed, which wasn't often, she looked comfortable and restrained, like an old armchair a kid could scramble over. But in bed she looked as if a man had just been there. Fran hated that.

"You were out all last night, Lee said."

Fran twisted the cap off one of the bottles and forced it on again. "Did he tell you why?"

Her mother's voice rose defensively. "I can't make him behave, Fran, you know I can't, not when I'm ill like this. You're old enough to be looking after yourselves now, anyway, you and Lee and Nigel. Why you have to make such a fuss about whose turn it is to clear up—"

"Because whoever's turn it is, it's never frigging Lee's!" Fran lowered her voice again. "I wish you'd tell him, Mom."

"I'm sick of telling him. I'm sick of telling all of you. I wish to God you'd go and live with your dad, all of you, and leave me in peace."

Fran looked at her. Her mother glared back with an expression of resentment, blame, and indefinite alarm. Her face was hard and red and shiny with sweat. There was a lot Fran thought of saying, but in the end all she said was: "I'm going to clear up now, anyhow."

"Well, that's something, then." Her mother lay back and let the empty mug drop from her fingers. Fran decided not to pick it up.

"Will you bring me something up, whoever's getting the tea?"

"All right."

As Fran reached the door, her mother said: "Where'd you go last night, anyway? Found yourself a boyfriend?"

"No," said Fran. "I just walked around."

"You be careful," her mother said. "I don't want you getting into any trouble."

"I can look after myself," Fran said, and slammed the door.

Downstairs she put the radio on and started in on the kitchen. She was full of energy and sang in a loud flat voice as she began to clear the things out of the sink. The water was only lukewarm, but she scraped away at the dishes and was happy to see them piling up on the kitchen table. After a while the water grew cold and she had to keep stopping to boil the kettle. There was a lot of crockery, as Mom had a habit of buying more to put off having to wash up. Fran thought for a minute of wiping out the cupboards, but that would mean taking everything out, so she just crammed the plates back in where she could. They had loads of stuff, Tupperware and cheap gadgets Mom had gotten out of the catalog. Nigel played with them sometimes. That was what Mom liked, shopping. She said it was the only thing that cheered her up. Even when she was really feeling bad and went to bed for days, she took the catalog with her so she could look at the pictures of nice things. "Stupid cow," said Fran aloud.

She decided to make some floor space by carrying the garbage bag out into the hall with the other one, but it split as she tried to shift it, spilling cans and cigarette ash and eggshells everywhere. So she sent Nigel out for more bags, and while she was waiting started to take the stove apart and chisel the grease out of the burners. She hadn't touched the stove for months and quickly realized it had been a mistake to try. By the time Nigel came back there was black stuff pushed right down under her nails, her fingers were sore, and her temper uncertain.

"What time is it?" she demanded.

Nigel got the clock for her to see.

"Shit!"

It was already four. That meant Lee would be home soon, demanding his tea. Fran felt rage rising up in her and started to bang the things around in the sink, splashing dirty water over the drainboard and onto the floor. She should have started in the living room instead. Or cleaned the bathroom. He wouldn't have come interrupting that. Nigel, quick to scent trouble, was sliding out into the hall.

"I don't know where you think you're going," Fran yelled.

"TV."

"Oh no, you don't."

But before she could think of something to make him do, the back door burst open. Lee was home.

A GIFT FOR A GIFT

•

He was thirteen, a tough undersized kid with a small scornful face and self-inflicted tattoos. When he saw Fran he grinned.

"A pal of mine said he saw you down the High Street last night, getting into some guy's car."

"He saw wrong then, didn't he."

"That's what I told him. No one'd stop to pick up our Fran, I said. Not with a face like hers."

Fran considered belting him, but she knew he could really hurt her if it came to a fight. So she picked up the broiling pan and rinsed it out.

"Did you go to school?" she asked.

"Mind your own business. Are you getting the tea?"

"With the gas stove in pieces? Looks like it, doesn't it?"

"Don't lose it," Lee said coolly. "I only asked. You're frigging touchy, Fran, do you know that? Like last night, going off. That's not normal."

Fran slammed down the broiling pan. "You'd know what's normal, would you, Lee? You think it's normal I should do everything around here while you sit staring at the goddamn TV!"

Lee shrugged. He went over to the bread box, pulled a slice out of the package, folded it, and stuffed it into his mouth.

"It's you that wants everything *nice*," he said indistinctly. "I don't give a shit what this place looks like. All I come back for is my tea, and if you're not here to get it, then I'll get it somewhere else. That's it, Fran. That's it, so you can stuff it." He pushed past Nigel and headed for the living room.

•

After a minute Nigel, with an uneasy glance at Fran, went to join him. Still standing at the sink, Fran heard the high edge of Nigel's laughter rise like a nervous scream above the noise of the TV. Lee was teasing him again, winding him up to the point where only a belting would bring him down. She hated Lee. She hated him. With exaggerated care she fitted the burners back onto the stove. The place still stank of stale grease. She picked up the garbage bag and hurled it into the hall. Then she sat down and stared at the tea-stained Formica tabletop. She was sick of trying to hold things together. She was ready to give up. The last time things got really bad was a year ago. Mom had gone into a mental hospital and the family had been taken into public assistance. Fran hadn't minded living at Nazareth House. The food was good, the rooms were kept clean, and the other kids had left her alone. Nigel had gone to foster parents and Lee to the council home, so she hadn't had to look after them. She had enjoyed the fixed routine of mealtimes and baths and prayers. It was like a holiday. It was like being a little kid again. No one expected her to be responsible for anything. One or two of the nuns seemed to like her, and the school she had been sent to had had a library. You could go there at dinnertime and read without any of the teachers passing remarks or the kids calling you a grind. She had almost begun to hope Mom would never be well enough to have her back.

Then when she was sent home, a few weeks later, Mom was so happy to see her Fran hated herself. Things didn't go too badly for the first few months. Someone had been in to clean the house and Mom had made a good stab at keeping things up. She did the shopping anyway, and went to rummage sales, bringing back bags full of clothes no one wanted to wear. The house was still stuffed full of Mom's bargains. Gradually, though, things started to slide. Mom couldn't manage on what she got from welfare and started buying little treats to cheer herself up. She didn't like to think about the state the house was getting into, so she got up later and later. Then the bills from the catalogs started arriving and she didn't get up at all. So Fran cashed the check every two weeks and tried to keep the money where Lee couldn't get at it, and regularly ran out a day or two before the next check was due. There were special meters for the gas and the electricity that paid a little off the old bills every time you put some money in, but that meant you hardly got any heat now. Nigel was always moaning about how cold it was. When any other bills came, Fran just tore them up and threw them in the wastebasket. She had nothing to pay them with.

Her dad had gotten sick of it years ago, and moved in with that cow Mrs. Thomas. Not that Fran really blamed him. She just missed him. For years after he left she had dreamed of him returning home and straightening everything out. Part of her still thought it might happen. Her earliest memory was of Dad laughing and holding her hand while she staggered into the sea. Though the wind whipped the hair across her face and the waves jostled her, she had known she was quite safe, her small hand lost in the warmth of his big one. When she thought of him she thought of good times. She could remember marching down High Street on Saturday afternoons with him and Lee, Dad pretending to be a millionaire able to buy them anything in sight. They would load him with presents to take home, presents for Mom and Nigel, presents for everyone. In the end Lee would get so excited he just jumped into Dad's arms, his face lit up like Nigel's. It hurt Fran to remember it. Lee had worshiped his dad. He never talked about him now.

"Fran?"

Nigel had reappeared in the doorway.

"What?" she snapped.

"Can't we have some tea? I'm starving."

Fran got reluctantly to her feet.

"I'll make some beans on toast. All right?"

"Again?" Nigel whined.

"Yes, again, and you'll goddamn well like it."

As Nigel flopped resentfully into a kitchen chair, Fran clipped him around the ear. He slid off the chair with a desolate wail and left the kitchen. She could hear him crying right down the hall. Tears pricked her eyes. She had to take it out on him, didn't she? Bad as goddamn Lee. Savagely she pulled out the broiling pan and began to slap pieces of bread in it.

Fran went to bed early that night and slept heavily, but not so heavily that Nigel didn't wake her as he scrambled into her bed, worming himself into the space between her body and the wall. She turned on her side to avoid contact with his sodden pajama bottoms. He was soon asleep again, but Fran lay with her eyes open, staring out at the glare of the streetlights through the thin curtains. Michael had asked her to come back.

CHAPTER THREE

THE NEXT MORNING, AFTER seeing Nigel off to school, Fran went back to the house. It was a long walk to the railroad bridge and by the time she got there she was edgy and afraid. She barely recognized the house. There was a dark bush growing close to the front windows that she did not remember, and the windows themselves were draped with ugly yellow netting. The place had a neglected look, like the house of an old woman who feeds stray cats and collects old newspapers in bundles. She stood on the bridge for a long time before going down.

When she reached the house she found the French windows unlocked as before, but the room beyond was empty. Fran stood among the birds in their rigid poses of flight or brooding and looking around her. There were holes in the dark red carpet and the chair covers were faded and worn. A clock on the mantelpiece disturbed the silence with its somber tick. She watched the dust spinning in a column of sunlight and wondered whether to go or stay. Eventually she went out into the hall. She called out quietly, but no one answered. Still she could not make up her mind to go. She lingered, looking at the paintings and noticing how the light fell in colored patches from the stained glass of the porch door. She liked this house. It was strange how different it seemed from the inside.

As she reached the stairs she heard a noise that seemed to come from the landing above.

"Michael?"

She began to climb, feeling excited and shy, but when she reached the landing she found it empty, and all the doors closed. She didn't know what to do then, so she went up to the nearest door and waited. After a few seconds the sound came again. It was laughter, unmistakably, coming from behind the door. It annoyed Fran. She swung open the door, expecting to catch Michael up to some trick. What she found was an old woman sitting up in bed, reading a paperback in a haze of cigarette smoke.

"Sorry, very sorry," Fran muttered, backing out.

But the old woman dropped her book and shouted: "Not so fast, young lady! Where do you think you're going?"

She had harsh brown hair, very frizzy and white at the roots. Her eyes were a milky blue and her face wizened as a monkey's, but Fran still recognized her.

"You're the woman in the photograph. You're the owner of the house." She was oddly shocked. In spite of the feeling of the house she hadn't expected the owner to be old. Fran's views of old people were decidedly mixed.

"I'm the owner," the old woman was agreeing rather dryly. "And who are you?"

"Deirdre," said Fran.

"Deirdre," she repeated, crushing her cigarette out onto a saucer full of stubs on the chair beside her. "And what made you decide to burgle my house, Deirdre? You're not carrying a bag marked loot, but I presume you've come for the silver."

She was so obviously unafraid that Fran felt both reassured and obscurely resentful.

"I'm not a burglar," she said, moving forward. "I wouldn't have told you my name if I was."

It looked as if the old girl was bedridden. A pile of books, a box of paper tissues, and what looked like a bottle of gin were all ranged within arm's length of her. Fran felt it was safe to go right up to the foot of the bed. The old woman continued to stare at her with the same undisturbed curiosity.

"If you're not a burglar," she said, "what do you want?"

Nettled, Fran replied with equal coolness: "Actually, I was looking for Michael."

The old woman's hands jerked violently in her lap. For a few moments she said nothing, but only looked at Fran. She was visibly shaken. "You've seen him?" she said at last.

Strange as Michael was, Fran thought this was stranger.

"I met him here, yesterday," she said. "I came in the back to get out of the rain and he was here."

"I don't understand you." The old woman was watching her narrowly.

"You called him and he came to you yesterday, do you mean? Or had you arranged to meet him here?"

"Called him?" Fran said. "We don't have a phone."

"You know perfectly well what I mean," she snapped. "You must have called him to you. He can't come unless he's called."

"I don't know what you're talking about," Fran said. "He lives in your house. I met him here."

"But it *can't* have been for the first time." She was losing her temper. "I tell you he can't come unless he's called. Even then he may not oblige. There must be thousands who have tried. How did you succeed, Deirdre? Were you dabbling in magic, or was it the pure cry of the heart?"

Fran backed toward the door.

"You're cracked," she said pityingly. "I hope there's someone looking after you."

"How can you be so stupid and so ignorant!" the old woman shouted. "If you are my successor, I shall tell Michael he has made a pretty poor choice."

"Tell him anything you like," Fran retorted. "Psychiatrist, is he?"

The old woman glared. "You have your hand on the doorknob," she said icily. "I suggest you use it."

That made it impossible for Fran to go. She turned and had a good slow look around the room. The furniture was heavy and dark, like the furniture downstairs, and the paint was yellowish with smoke and age. But there was a fresh breeze from the open window and the room was clean in spite of its clutter of books and newspapers. Fran went over to the dressing table and ran a finger over the polished wood.

"Who does the dusting for you? Michael?"

The old woman pressed her lips together and did not reply. Fran opened a jewelry box and ran her fingers through the tangled necklaces inside. Any minute now, she thought, I'm going to do something really crazy.

"Deirdre." The old woman's voice, breaking the silence, lowered the tension a little. "If you came to my house yesterday as you say, what brought you here? Please don't waste my time with lies. Did you really not know that you would be meeting Michael?"

Fran snapped the jewelry box shut.

"I wanted to come in," she said without turning around. "I don't know why. But I think it was the house, not Michael. I kept thinking he didn't seem to fit. It's different, the feeling that brought me here, and the feeling about him."

She did not know why she wanted to say it, but she added:

"But you're right, I did call him. At least, I called someone. I didn't know it would be him."

"The house and Michael," the woman said. "My house and Michael. So we both drew you here."

"Yes."

Fran felt so exposed it came out in a whisper.

Then the old woman giggled. It was a sly, almost gloating sound. Disturbed, Fran turned around. The old woman grinned at her. "Michael won't like that," she said. "He'll be expecting to have you to himself."

"Tell me about him," Fran demanded.

"All right," said the old woman, still grinning. "But you must make me a cup of tea first. I'm simply *gasping*."

Fran was glad to have a few minutes alone. She took her time in the kitchen, choosing cups instead of mugs and even hunting out a tray cloth. The milk smelled doubtful, but she put it in a jug anyway. When the tray was ready it looked beautiful. On impulse, Fran took everything off again and removed the cloth. She had no confidence in her ability to please. Besides, she hadn't really decided if she wanted to please or not.

"Tea, how nice. And cookies!" The old woman's eyes lit up greedily. "Clear that chair for the tray, Deirdre, and bring up another for yourself. That's right."

Fran wished she had thought of something better than Deirdre, but she was stuck with it now.

"You haven't told me your name," she said.

"It's Hilary. Hilary Stock." The old woman bit into a cookie and added with her mouth full: "I was a schoolteacher before I retired. Don't you go in for it. It's a rotten job."

"I'll try not to," said Fran, keeping a straight face. She poured the tea. Neither of them seemed able to find an easy way to continue the conversation. When they did speak it was both at once.

"Where do you—"

"How long have you—"

"Please," said Hilary. "You first."

"I was just going to ask how long you've known Michael."

"We've known each other since I was a child."

"Shit!"

Fran had spilled hot tea all down her sweater.

"That wouldn't happen if you held the cup properly," Hilary observed. "Did I startle you?"

Fran looked at her. Then she laughed. "You goddamn well know you did," she said.

Hilary winced just perceptibly.

"But he can't be that old," Fran said. "He only looks about thirty."

"My dear, what exactly do you know about him?"

Fran was reluctant to give up the little she knew before Hilary had told her anything, but she could hardly refuse. "He made the birds downstairs come alive," she said rather sullenly. "And he knew my name before I told him."

"His best parlor magic," Hilary murmured. "He likes you. Did he tell you that Eternity is in love with the products of time?"

"That's Blake," said Fran, and could have bitten her tongue off.

Hilary's face lit up. "Do you know Blake? That's marvelous. I didn't know he was taught in schools."

"He isn't," Fran muttered. "Not in mine. I just read that stuff sometimes."

"I'm glad to hear it. It's only a step from the strangeness of poetry to the strangeness of real life."

"Real life isn't strange," Fran said patronizingly. "It's too goddamn predictable."

"Michael isn't strange?"

"All right." Fran banged her cup down on the tray. "You win. Now tell me about him."

Hilary settled herself back against her pillows and lit a cigarette. Clearly she meant to enjoy herself.

"As I told you," she began, "I first met Michael in childhood. I suppose I was about fourteen. To understand what happened, you need to know a little about my family, especially my father. That's him, over there." Fran looked at the photograph on the wall. It showed a stout, unsmiling man with a heavy mustache and not much hair.

"There were only the two of us," Hilary said. "My mother died when I was very small. I don't remember her. But my father never got over her death. He was a very quiet man, shut up in himself and hard to talk to. He taught Classics at the boys' grammar school, but he didn't enjoy his teaching and I don't think he was at all popular. What he lived for was birds."

"Birds?"

"You know, ornithology. Birdwatching. He used to write articles for journals and endless letters to *The Times*. The specimens downstairs are his, of course."

"I suppose you liked birds too," Fran said, beginning to get a little bored.

"Goodness, no." Hilary blew out smoke. "I hated them. I used to lie in bed and pretend I had St. Patrick's power of cursing, so that when I got up in the morning they'd all be gone. Silence and empty skies. Nothing for Daddy to look at but me."

She spoke with such force of emotion that Fran was embarrassed.

"You talk as if it still matters."

Hilary took a long look at her.

"You don't know many old people, do you?" she said. "Not outside the zoos they call old people's homes, I mean."

"No," said Fran. She thought of her grandmother down in Bournemouth, last seen four years ago. "No, I don't know anyone old, not really."

"Then don't imagine feelings age and shrink like bodies," Hilary said. "Feelings stay. What goes is the pretense that time makes a difference. I'm too old to pretend now and too tired to be polite. I suppose that's why the old are shut up. They lose all restraint. And then one's forced to see that underneath, nothing's been resolved, nothing's been learned." Fran felt even more uncomfortable after this speech. It must have shown in her face, for Hilary said: "I'm sorry. We were talking about my father, weren't we?"

"You were," said Fran. But she liked the old girl really, so she added: "It's interesting. I like to hear about people's childhoods."

"Do you?" Hilary looked at her doubtfully. "It's true that it's often the most interesting part of a *book*. . . . But in my case it was horribly dull. They say, don't they, that childhood flies fast? Mine didn't. It crawled. Some afternoons during school vacations I used to think time had stuck. My father spent all his time between his meals in his study. He didn't like to be disturbed and he certainly didn't want the noise and fuss of other children in the house. I was expected to amuse myself quietly and not be a nuisance."

"You must have been lonely," Fran said.

"I was desperate. I can see now that my father simply had no idea of the needs of a child, but at the time I thought I was being punished for something. I thought he hated me. He didn't know how to talk to me, you see. At mealtimes he would ask about my health and my lessons with the heavy politeness of a visitor, and then bury himself thankfully in his newspaper. It was awful! Then one day when I was about thirteen, I discovered the reasons for his behavior toward me. I found out that I had killed my mother."

"You *what*?"

Hilary evidently enjoyed the reaction her words produced.

"Oh, I don't mean deliberately," she said. "I mean it was my birth that killed her. In those days it was a lot commoner than it is now. She was never strong, and she caught some infection that, in the absence of antibiotics, carried her off. I overheard some relatives discussing it at a family funeral. They were talking about how much her death had changed my father. If it wasn't for me, they said, she would still be alive."

"But of course they didn't mean—" Fran began, but she was interrupted.

"No, but think how it felt! My father had lost my mother,

whom he adored, and I was the cause. I knew I could never make it up to him but somehow I had to try. My mother had been a clever woman, as well as a pretty one. There was nothing I could do about my face, but I began to work very hard at school. With a lot of hard work I started to come second or third in just about everything but Latin, my father's subject. Somehow that always defeated me. He didn't notice the change immediately, of course. But when I brought him my report at the end of that school year I felt certain he would be pleased."

"And was he?"

Hilary looked away. She spoke slowly, as if to control the pain the memory still gave her. "He read through the report without saying a word. Then at the end he handed it back to me and said: 'You realize, Hilary, that the only subject really worth mastering is Classics. And that really isn't a subject for girls.' "

"What the—"

Fran caught Hilary's expression and restrained herself. "Sorry. But what made him say that?"

"I don't know. I really don't. I think he was trying to tell me not to bother, that nothing would ever change the way he felt. The love wasn't there, and that was that. But of course I couldn't accept that. I knew I had to make him love me, somehow. So I knew I had to excel in Latin."

"You should have given up," Fran said. "I would."

"Well—" Hilary smiled. "We could argue about that another time. The point is, I was desperate. I didn't know what to do. I tried to work by myself over the summer, but when school started it became obvious that I was just as bad at Latin as ever. The end of term exams were coming up and our teacher, Miss Baines, was a tartar. I knew I couldn't ask her for help. There was no one I could turn to."

"So what did you do?"

"I turned to magic."

CHAPTER FOUR

"Magic?"

Before Hilary could say any more, the door opened. It was Michael. Fran felt a small cold shock at seeing him. He looked so solidly ordinary as he came toward them, a little taller and a little fatter than she remembered. She noticed how fine his brown hair was, and how the skin around his eyes crinkled as he smiled. He did not speak to her, but looked inquiringly at Hilary. She said: "I gather you've already met Deirdre."

"I certainly have."

Fran's eyes met his. He winked.

"Actually," Fran said, clearing her throat, "Deirdre's my middle name. The one I mostly use is Fran. Fran Kelly."

"I see," said Hilary.

"You ought to," Michael said. "You haven't always found it convenient to use your own name."

"I don't think Fran wants to hear about that," Hilary said sharply.

A GIFT FOR A GIFT

"Really?" Michael smiled. "Just as you like."

He began to pick up the scattered newspapers, folded them neat and small, then knelt down and pushed them under the bed. Fran could see the space was already tightly packed.

"It's Hilary's funeral pyre," Michael said. "She wants to burn like the phoenix."

"Don't fantasize," snapped Hilary. "You know I keep them in case there's something I want to reread."

"Come on now," said Michael. "Don't you think the fantasy's yours?" He turned to Fran.

"She should really be in a hospital. She's outlived her family and quarreled with all her friends, so when the doctor told her she couldn't go on living alone, she pretended she was moving south to her sister's family. They haven't caught up with her yet. She wanted to sit it out alone, but of course I wasn't going to let that happen."

"Of course not," Hilary said sourly. "Imagine you letting me die in peace."

Fran knew she should say something sympathetic, but she couldn't find the words.

"Even if you could, I don't suppose she'd want to hear them," Michael said.

"That's enough showing off," Hilary said nastily.

"Maybe Fran likes me to show off," Michael retorted.

Fran was getting a bit sick of this. "I don't need you to speak for me," she said to Michael. "I've got a tongue in my head. And I'm not mental, either."

"So sorry," said Michael, grinning. "And how were you

37

employing your tongues, the two of you, before I came and interrupted?"

"I was telling Fran how I met you," Hilary said.

"How flattering. But there's no need, is there, now that I'm here to tell her myself. Too much talk tires you out, Hilary. At least that's what you tell me whenever I want to talk to you."

"As you like."

Hilary's tone was indifferent, but as she sat back and lit another cigarette, Fran thought she looked anything but pleased.

Michael went over to the dressing table and began to clear the things off it.

"Why are you doing that?" asked Fran.

"You'll see."

He began to sweep his hand over the mirror. At first Fran could see no difference, but as his fingers passed lower and lower she realized that he was somehow wiping away the reflection of the room. Bed, chairs, and faces had disappeared, but the mirror was not left empty. Tiny figures appeared instead, very bright and active, but too small for Fran to see.

"What is it?" she demanded.

"Wait."

Michael stepped back from the dressing table and held up his hand. Slowly he began to lower it, closing his fingers, pulling the air in toward him like a cloth. As Fran watched him she realized something strange was happening to the light. The edges of the room were growing dark and the area around Michael was getting brighter and brighter, too bright for her to look at. It wasn't air he was pulling in, it was the light. He gathered it into his hand, and shut his fingers over it. Fran could see the cracks between his fingers glowing like fire in the dark. The mirror was like a movie screen in the darkened room, and now there came voices, but so loud and fuzzy that Fran could not make out what they were saying.

"I still don't—"

"Quiet, Fran!"

The figures were outgrowing the mirror. They were standing in the room now and somehow it was the room that was growing smaller, receding and becoming invisible, and Fran with it. She could no longer see herself, and yet she was still there to see and hear. Closest to her was a girl with braids in a dressing gown. The girl was standing in front of a fire and there was something in her hand. It glittered as her hand moved. She said: "The best I have. A gift for a gift, a favor for a favor." She threw it forward, and as she did so, it seemed to Fran as though a volume switch was being turned up, a switch affecting not sound, but feelings and sensations. Fran knew what the girl knew. The bedroom fire was hot on her face and she was sweating slightly under the heavy red dressing gown. The brooch her mother had left her was blackening in the flames of the fire, but nothing had happened. No help had come. She felt a little sick as she repeated: "A favor for a favor." Then more urgently: "Come! Please come!"

Nothing happened. No one claimed it. She watched the flames die down and the brooch remain, stubbornly wedged among the coals. Of course she had known nothing would happen. She felt cold and silly and unexpectedly relieved.

There was a moment of darkness, then the girl appeared again. It was morning and she was kneeling in front of the cold grate, stirring the ashes with the poker. The brooch was not there. She plunged her hands into the ashes, kneading with her fingers and making a terrible mess, but still she couldn't find it. It hadn't slipped down between the bars. It had gone. She didn't know what to do, she was so frightened.

The girl was at breakfast now, unable to eat.

"Everything all right, Hilary?"

Her father glanced up from his newspaper. She didn't know what to say.

"Daddy—" she began. He looked up with such obvious patience that she couldn't continue. "Nothing. It doesn't matter."

She was in a classroom now, sitting close to the front. Her fear mixed with all the other fear in the room and lost its special quality. As the teacher went up and down the rows, slapping a paper down on each desk, Hilary almost laughed with relief. The Latin looked as difficult as ever. That brooch must just have slipped out of the grate somehow.

The other girls sucked their pens and began to write. The teacher slid her library book onto her lap and a peppermint into her mouth. The smell of it made Hilary look up. She nearly screamed. There was a man standing behind Miss

Baines. He was dressed in a black suit and had a reddish beard. Pinned to his lapel was her brooch. He smiled at her and raised his hand slightly in greeting. Then he began to write on the board. Hilary turned her head. The other girls were bent over their work or searching for inspiration out of the window. Couldn't anyone else see him or what he was writing? She fiddled with her pen. This wasn't the kind of help she had really meant. This smacked of cheating. But she had already seen some of the answers, so she would be cheating whatever happened. The man had finished writing now, and turned to look at her. She had a feeling he knew what was going through her mind. Strangely enough that didn't frighten her. He bowed a little ironically, and was gone. After a few seconds she uncapped her pen and began to write.

As she ran out of school at the end of the afternoon, someone caught her by the arm. It was the man. He smiled, and said: "A gift for a gift, and a favor for a favor. But I should be allowed to choose, don't you think?"

He unpinned the brooch and pressed it into her hand.

"Michael!"

Hilary's voice brought sudden darkness. "Don't you think that's enough? You're surely not going to make Fran ride piggyback through the rest of my life?"

"She'd find it most instructive. All the same . . ." Light spilled out of Michael's hand back into the room.

Fran's eyes hurt and everything in the room seemed unreal.

She was afraid to look at Hilary. She felt very close to her and yet horribly ashamed, like a Peeping Tom.

"Not to worry, Fran," said Michael with callous cheerfulness. "It's just a trick."

At that moment Fran hated him. She reached out and touched Hilary's hand. "What happened after that?"

"After that?" Hilary looked shaken. "After that I went on to specialize in Classics, relying on Michael's help. I went to college and thought of becoming a professor, but ambition failed me and I went to teach in a girls' school instead. Eventually, my father became ill and I came home and lived with him until he died."

"Not before I had disentangled you from one or two small messes," Michael said.

Hilary did not look at him.

"She had a weakness for clever young men," Michael said. "Still has. I think that's why she's so fond of me."

"What happened with your father?" Fran asked Hilary.

"Nothing very much," she replied quietly. "The only comment he ever made about my career was to ask when I was going to marry and have a family. I never did. And when he was dying, one of the last things he said to me was a joke about dried-up spinsters. He never said—well, you know."

There was a silence. Then Hilary smiled wryly. "Michael gave me what I asked for. It's hardly his fault it didn't have the effect I wanted."

"Of course it isn't," said Michael. "And you can't say my terms are unreasonable."

A GIFT FOR A GIFT

"Terms?" Fran didn't understand.

"A gift for a gift," Michael repeated.

"That's between ourselves," Hilary said sharply.

"You don't want Fran to learn anything, do you?" Michael said teasingly. "Oh, well. I expect she and I will come to our own agreement. If she stays. You are staying, Fran? To lunch, at least?"

Fran looked at Hilary, who nodded.

"Yes, please," Fran said.

Michael made a sardonic little bow, and left the room.

Fran felt most of the tension leave the room with him. She said rather flippantly: "Does he cook or does he just magic it out of the air?"

"He cooks," said Hilary. "He even shops. He can't make something out of nothing. He can only manipulate things a little, like a high-class conjuror. So don't let him fool you, Fran."

Fran thought this rather grudging after what they had just seen. "Who is he, then?" she demanded.

"Ask him. I'm sure he'll be delighted to tell you. Perhaps you'll understand it better than I did. All I really grasped was that he isn't a human being."

Fran attempted to absorb this without too much show of surprise.

Hilary went on: "I feel I should warn you against him, Fran. You'll get no joy by him. It's a kind of addiction, life with Michael. The pleasure gets smaller and smaller, and you can see the time of payment approaching, but still you can't get free."

"I haven't asked him for anything yet," Fran said rather resentfully. "And he hasn't offered."

"He will though," Hilary said. "And do you really imagine you'll turn him down? You've drawn him to you because you're reckless, open to anything. You've let him in, Fran. I don't think you'll send him away." Fran said nothing. She wanted to tell Hilary to mind her own business, but she couldn't quite manage it.

"You're my successor," Hilary said rather sadly. "But it's curious there should be an overlap. I suppose there were others before me, but I certainly never met them." She looked at Fran meditatively. "You were drawn to my house as well as to Michael. I wonder why."

Fran shrugged. "Dunno," she said and smiled, a little embarrassed by Hilary's serious stare.

"Stay with me," Hilary said abruptly. "Come and stay. Could you?"

Fran couldn't believe it. She didn't dare say anything.

"Of course you can't." Hilary pulled a disappointed face. "You have a family. You're needed at home."

"No," said Fran slowly. "I wouldn't say that." She crushed the thought of Nigel. "I can do what I like. But you don't want me here."

Hilary laughed at that. "I'm a selfish old woman," she said. "It's because I'm selfish that I want you here. But will you come all the same?"

Fran took a deep breath. "Yes," she said.

"That's settled, then. I'm so glad. I'll have Michael make

up a bed for you. And you'll want to go home to collect some things and to explain."

Hilary sat back looking exhausted. The skin of her face was loose and yellowish and there were deep black rings under her eyes. Fran was suddenly scared by the thought of how old and ill she was.

"I won't be any trouble," Fran said.

Hilary grinned. "I wish I could promise the same."

CHAPTER FIVE

WHEN FRAN GOT HOME at about three o'clock she went straight upstairs to pack. There was only one suitcase in the house, the large red one Mom used when she went to the hospital. Fran got it down from on top of the cupboard on the landing and flung dirty clothes and her books and a couple of tapes into it. There wasn't much she wanted to take, but she wasn't going to take it in a plastic garbage bag like she had to Nazareth House. When she had finished she sat down on the floor and hugged her knees. She was going to break her promise and hurt Nigel terribly. It wasn't fair, it was wrong, but she knew she was still going to do it. "You're a hard cow, Fran Kelly," she said aloud. But saying it didn't change anything.

Eventually she got up and went to her mother's room. The bed was empty, the covers thrown back and the bottom sheet awry, exposing the mattress. Fran shut the door on it and went downstairs to the living room. There she found her mother, watching television in her pink nylon housecoat and eating pineapple chunks out of a can.

"You feeling better, Mom?"

"A bit." Her mother didn't take her eyes off the screen. "Sit down, can't you? You make me nervous, fidgeting."

Fran didn't move. "Mom——" She didn't know how to begin to say it.

"Oh, *what*?" Her mother banged the tablespoon into the empty can and set it on the floor. She still wouldn't turn around. "Aren't you supposed to be at school instead of bothering the life out of me?"

"Goddamn it!"

Fran threw herself into a chair and waited for the film to end.

At last, when doctor and nurse were united in an embrace against an improbable African sunset, Fran got up and tried again.

"Mom?"

"Yes, please, love."

Fran was baffled. "Yes please what?"

Her mother blinked in surprise. "Aren't you putting the kettle on? I thought that's what you meant."

"I will in a minute," Fran said. "But listen, Mom, will you? This is something important."

"Mmm?"

Her mother still had more than half her attention on the commercials. Fran raised her voice. "There's these two friends of mine. People I've met. They've offered me—well, the woman's offered, it's her house—she said I could go and live there if I wanted. And I want to."

Her mother stared in silence at Captain Birdseye and his crew of happy youngsters. Fran added: "You said you wanted us to go. So I'm going. All right?"

Her mother slewed around, panic and resentment in her eyes. "All right?" she said. "All right? Who's going to look after the boys? Who's going to look after Nigel?"

Fran felt sick. "He'll have to take his chances."

Guilt flared into anger at the look on her mother's face.

"He's not my kid, for Christ's sake!" she shouted. "It's your job to look after him. It's about time I got the chance to do what *I* want."

"But you're his sister!"

"So?" Fran retorted with a coolness she was far from feeling.

Her mother's face reddened. She fiddled with a button of her housecoat.

"I rely on you," she said. "Fran."

"But it's no good, Mom," Fran said, fighting tears. "I do a rotten job. Lee hates me. Nigel's running wild. Things can't get worse. They can't. And it isn't fair."

"But this is your home, Fran!" her mother wailed.

"Yes," said Fran fiercely. "And look at it."

Her mother's expression changed. "It's a man," she said in a hard tight voice. "It's a man, I know it is."

"Mom—" Fran began desperately, but her mother spoke louder.

"You're still underage, you know. I'll have the police on to him. All that rubbish about a couple."

"For God's sake, Mom!" Fran felt disgusted. "You've got men on the frigging brain. I told you, it's a woman. There isn't a man anywhere near the place."

"You said a couple!" Her mother looked at her triumphantly. "I know when you're lying, young lady, so you needn't—"

"He isn't a man."

Her mother stopped short and stared at her. Fran slowly turned red. "You can think what you like," she said in a thin high voice. "Think what you goddamn like. I'm going anyway." She turned and ran out of the room.

Upstairs she threw herself onto the bed. She hated her mother for making her feel ashamed. She had never thought of Michael that way. Had she? But there was no time really to face the question. She must leave before Nigel came home from school, or she wouldn't have the nerve to leave at all. She picked up the suitcase and went out onto the landing. Through the open door she could see that Mom had gone back to bed.

"I'm off now," she called.

There was no answer from her mother's room.

A few hours later she was sitting in Hilary's kitchen eating a meal Michael had cooked. The food was delicious; Fran would have felt less treacherous if it had been terrible. She ate slowly and self-consciously, aware of Michael across the table, resting his chin on folded arms and watching her with attentive brown eyes. She did not feel comfortable sitting alone with him.

"Penny for them," he said eventually.

Fran did not look up.

"I was just wondering what the others had for tea."

"French fries, I expect."

Fran pulled a face.

"Don't feel guilty," Michael said. "Your good luck didn't make theirs bad."

Fran wasn't so sure. She raised her eyes to his face. "Hilary said I should ask you about yourself. She told me you weren't human. I should have guessed it from the way you talk."

He sat back, taking the pinprick seriously.

"You think I'm heartless? Hardly a rare quality among humans."

"So where do you come from?" Fran grinned. "Outer space?"

Michael's mouth twitched. "Is that the limit of your imagination? Oh, Fran."

Chagrined, she pushed away her half-full plate.

"I'm not actually that interested," she said coldly. "It was only that Hilary told me to ask."

"Come on," he said. She could tell he was smiling. "Admit it. You're dying to know."

"Oh, *dying*," she repeated sarcastically. But she couldn't hold out against his smile. Almost against her will, the muscles of her face relaxed into a grin.

"Good," he said. "I can tell you now."

But he didn't, not at once. He went on looking at her, stroking the beard around his mouth with thick, rather short fingers.

"It's difficult to explain," he said at last. "I don't remember all of it very clearly. It goes too far back. But I was *outside*, Fran. I don't remember how I got there, but that's where I was."

"Outside what?"

"Outside everything. It isn't a place. The word 'place' has no meaning there. It's a disturbance, a darkness, somewhere that shouldn't be. I was there, alone and cold in the dark, when somebody opened a door and I came here."

He smiled like a child. "I like it here," he said. "It's warm. Things happen. People like what I do for them. They stay with me, and that makes the cold a little easier to bear."

Fran could not make sense of this. "I thought you left the cold when you came here," she said.

Michael looked annoyed. "I told you it wasn't a place," he said. "Don't you understand? It's in you as much as you're in it. You carry it inside you, and you can't leave it, not really. You can only make it easier to bear." He hesitated, then he added: "At least, there is a way, but it's too terrible. I don't even want to think about that."

Fran looked at him, troubled. It sounded like madness, but he spoke so simply she believed him. "And was it Hilary that opened the door?"

"No. That happened a long time ago. But I was glad to come to Hilary when she called." He added with a ghost of his familiar grin, "She's had the benefit of an old-fashioned education. She knew what she was doing. We very quickly came to an understanding."

"But I didn't know I was calling you," Fran said.

"No," Michael agreed. "But you gave me the opportunity to reach you all the same. And because you didn't know what you were seeking, I expect you've given the same opportunity to other forces. An open invitation, if you like."

Fran didn't like. She stood up and reached for her plate. As she did so, she was arrested by a mental image so powerful that for a moment she lost all sense of where she was. She saw a bird descending out of light, wings spread like flame as if to burn her. It was gone in a moment, but the noise that accompanied it, a roaring like wind or fire, stayed in her ears. She turned to Michael in terror.

"What is it, Fran?" he demanded, seizing her arm. "What's the matter?" She shook her head. She could not speak. The image or daylight dream, whatever it was, had left her feeling vulnerable and sick. And though she dreaded the thought of it returning, she felt at the same time a strange loneliness now that it had gone. It was so beautiful.

Michael looked at her thoughtfully for a while, then picked up her plate.

"I can see we will have to be careful," he said. "But let's wash up now, shall we?"

Fran was glad of something practical to do, and grateful to Michael for letting her alone while she recovered. As they were drying up she felt like talking again, but not about what she had just seen. She wanted to forget that if she could.

"If you're not human, Michael," she said, reverting to the earlier conversation, "how come you look like us?"

"That's just for your benefit."

"You mean you can take any shape you want?"

"More or less. I don't have any particular shape I recognize as myself in the way you do. I don't really have a body, not in the sense you have."

"Then don't you find it a little cramped? I mean, we're used to being stuck in a body, but if you can manage without one—"

"Mine's elastic," Michael said.

Suddenly he was gone. When he spoke again his voice was tickling her ear, small and vibrant as an insect's hum, though she couldn't see him at all.

"They used to argue about how many angels could dance on the point of a pin. Careful, now, Fran, don't scratch yourself or I'll be in trouble. The answer"—his voice had moved farther away—"the answer, as you can see, is as many as cared to do anything so silly."

Fran felt something on her hand. Looking down she saw it was Michael, half an inch tall, capering about like a cartoon elf. She disliked the sensation so much she had a strong impulse to shake him onto the floor. He was too small for her to see his face, but she was sure he was laughing at her. She held herself rigid and waited for him to get bored.

"In any case"—his body was soon back at the sink again—"you shouldn't speak of yourself with such disrespect. Stuck in a body indeed. Don't you know what you are?"

Fran was getting annoyed. "Why don't you just tell me?"

"It's not my business."

Fran scowled at him. "So what is your business, Michael? What do you want me for?"

Michael smiled his most beautiful smile.

"Eternity is in love with the products of time."

"Hilary told me you'd say that," Fran jeered.

Michael's smile disappeared.

"Hilary would," he said sulkily.

"It's no answer anyway," Fran said.

Michael reached out and touched her very lightly under the chin.

"Isn't it?" he said.

Fran felt herself turn scarlet.

"It's my pleasure to give you what you want," Michael said. "Anything, Fran."

CHAPTER SIX

FRAN GOT AWAY SOMEHOW. She went up to her room, un-dressed, and got into bed mechanically. Of course, she couldn't sleep. She kept going over what Michael had said, how he had looked when he touched her, until the memory was as dry and flavorless as a sucked orange. Then she began to think about what she might ask him to do, the thousands of things she wanted and now could have. Her mind grew more and more fevered, as if she had been given a million pounds to spend and an hour to spend it in. Eventually she sat up and put on the light. She felt ashamed and sickened at herself.

The alarm clock on the bedside table told her it was just past midnight. She wondered whether Nigel was asleep yet. She missed his knees digging into her back. There was nothing in the room to compensate for his absence. It was large and cold and very quiet; the shadows from the heavy furniture were deep and solemn and there was no noise from the street.

Michael had told her this room had belonged to Hilary's father, and his clothes still hung in the big wardrobe. They were his books, too, in the little bookcase between the bed and the wall. Fran leaned over and had a look at them. There were shabby copies of Greek plays she could not read, books about cricket, a Bible, and a large bound volume of a magazine called *The Ornithologist*. Fran lifted it out and began to turn over the pages. Every third or fourth article had been written by Charles Stock, M.A., Hilary's father. Fran felt a shock of recognition every time she saw the name. Eventually she shut the book and just held it. It was the first time she had ever felt a direct contact with a writer. Though the link was slight and the subject matter outside her, it still struck Fran with extraordinary force: there weren't just words, there were people writing them. And if she could ask Michael for anything in the world—

Suddenly she threw the book across the room, denting the heavy pages against the wall.

"Crap!" she said aloud in a voice harsh with self-hatred. "It's a load of crap. Even with Michael you wouldn't have a hope." All the same she had to get away from the idea of it. She got out of bed and went to the door, then stopped. If she went downstairs to the kitchen to make herself some tea, would she find Michael there, sitting in the dark like an unattended machine, waiting for the return of daylight and company? The thought was horrible. She changed her mind about the kitchen, and decided to go and see if Hilary was awake.

●

She crossed the landing quietly and eased open Hilary's door, afraid to knock in case the old girl really was asleep. But it was all right.

"Who's there?" Hilary called at once.

"Me." Fran came toward the bed. "I couldn't sleep. I thought I'd see if you were awake too."

"I often am at night." Hilary put on the bedside lamp and lit a cigarette. Her face looked grayish and strained, as if she was in pain.

"Aren't you cold?" she said, staring at the big T-shirt Fran wore to bed. "Why don't you take the quilt off the bed and wrap yourself up in it?" Fran did so, tucking her feet under her in the chair beside the bed. For a while neither spoke, each thinking her own thoughts. Then Fran said: "You didn't use Michael's power much, did you?"

Hilary roused herself. "What do you mean?"

Fran hesitated. "Well, becoming a teacher. And living in your father's house. It's not very—"

"Exciting?" Hilary smiled to herself. "You may remember I got Michael to leave out the exciting parts. I had my share of adventures. As I told you, Michael's addictive. But I've never been ambitious and I haven't many passions, whatever Michael likes to pretend. What drove me in the beginning was desperation about my father. I don't think I've felt anything as strong as that in the whole of the rest of my life."

Fran had another question. "And couldn't Michael make him love you?"

Hilary snorted. "I never asked him."

"Why not?"

"Don't you see? It wouldn't have been *him,* Fran. It would have been Michael. And what would that have been worth? My present to myself, that's all." She ground out her cigarette. "What I tried to do was foolish enough, and perhaps it's just as well that I didn't succeed."

Fran picked at a loose thread on the quilt and said quite casually: "But did you get everything you asked for really, then?"

Hilary wasn't fooled. She looked shrewdly at Fran.

"Are you trying to decide what to do? My child, I can't possibly advise you. I'm what they call an interested party. For my own sake I don't want to warn you against him, though I know I should. But you have to realize you'll pay a price all your life and then—"

She broke off and her tone changed. In a rapid and flippant voice she went on: "What do you want to do with Michael, anyway, that you couldn't do for yourself? Travel around the world? Become Prime Minister? You're clever enough to do all that under your own steam, surely?"

Fran found this very offensive. She thought Hilary could be a really snotty bitch sometimes. In a flat sullen voice she said: "Without Michael I'll leave school as soon as I'm sixteen and try to enter a training program."

"Is that what you want?"

"What's that got to do with it?" Fran retorted. "What else is there?"

Hilary did not hesitate. "You're a bright girl. Why don't you stay on and take college-entrance exams?"

"College-entrance exams!" It was so absurd Fran had trouble finding an answer. Eventually she said: "For a start, I haven't been going to school very much recently. You can't just take college-entrance exams, you know. You've got to take SATs and the teachers have to think you're up to it and all that. I'm in the rubbish class. They know I'm rubbish." She was beginning to get upset. "And anyway, they don't pay you to stay on."

"I see."

Fran recognized that tone very well. Her anger rose to it. "No, you don't! You think I'm a lazy cow, don't you? You think I can't be bothered. All anyone need do is try, isn't that it, and they're bound to be better off? Well, I've seen the ones that tried. They're in the same boat as the ones that never bothered. They just have longer faces, that's all."

Hilary put out her hand in placatory appeal.

"That's not what I meant," she said. "I used to be a teacher, remember? I hate waste—I've seen too much of it. You're too bright to go to waste, Fran. No doubt if I knew your friends at school I might say the same of them, but it's you I know. You say that without Michael you'll achieve nothing, but I don't think that's true. And how will you feel about anything you do achieve if it's through him? Will you be proud of yourself, Fran? Will you? Or will you know it's all a sham and a cheat and wonder just what you might have done if you'd tried on your own?"

"I did try," Fran said. She spoke in such a low voice Hilary had to lean forward to catch it. "You talk about your dad. At least he noticed what you did. I used to be quite good in school till I realized no one gave a shit whether I was good or not. I can still remember when the penny finally dropped. I was in middle school. I had a poem put up on the wall. Miss Bonner's class, that was. I liked her, I didn't mind working hard for her. Anyhow, my poem was put up on the wall for Parents' Night. It was a good poem and I wanted Mom to see it up there. I told her, and she said she'd go, but she didn't. Neither of them went, not ever. So Miss Bonner took down the poem and gave it to me to take home."

"And was your mother pleased?"

"She never saw it. I tore it up on the way home and poked it down a drain."

Hilary did not speak, but reached out a mottled hand and touched Fran's briefly.

"I stopped trying after that," Fran said. "So you needn't think it'd bother me to use Michael. I'm not interested in what I can do by myself. It's too late for that."

"I see." Hilary stared ahead as if making a calculation. "So do you think you are willing to pay the price for using Michael?"

"What's that, then?" Fran demanded truculently, though her eyes glittered and she was having to blink rapidly to keep back the tears.

"Firstly, you'll be lonely," said Hilary. "You may start off thinking you can have Michael and a lot of other things, but in the end all you'll have is Michael. By accepting his help you begin to move into his world. And you'll find it impossible to be close to other people or to explain to them about him. For one thing he doesn't like it, and for another they won't believe you. And however much you may come to want to get rid of him, however bored and weary you become, you'll find it can't be done. The habit is too strong, and besides, you've promised."

"Promised what?"

"Not to leave him. Though he's as bored and weary as you are, he'll hold you to your promise, because he can't bear to be alone."

It still didn't sound too bad to Fran. She grinned. "Like being married, do you mean?"

"Not like being married. Marriage ends with death."

Fran looked at her in astonishment. "You have to stay with Michael after you're dead?"

"That's the bargain. That's the only gift he will accept."

"From me too?"

Hilary smiled sourly. "You're young and fresh and entertaining. I'm sure he thinks you'd be good company."

Fran didn't know what to think of that. She found it hard to think of herself as dead, let alone as being good company after the event.

"You haven't taken anything from him yet," Hilary said.

"No," said Fran. "Not yet." She looked at Hilary in some confusion and embarrassment. "But would it really be so terrible to have to stay with him?" she asked.

Something like a groan escaped from Hilary. "I've done my best," she said. "You must choose for yourself, Fran—but not tonight. It's time you went back to bed. School tomorrow, remember."

"School?" Fran pulled a face and yawned. "You're joking!"

"While you live under my roof you'll go," Hilary said. "It's a matter of principle."

Fran swore under her breath. But she didn't really mind. "All right," she said, and grinned. "Seeing it's you, I will."

CHAPTER SEVEN

THE BIOLOGY LAB STANK. The cages where the rats were kept needed cleaning out again. Fran was sitting close to them and far from the windows; she was drowsy and thirsty and full of shepherd's pie and French fries. It was the first class of the afternoon and it gave her the same feeling as a television program she couldn't be bothered to turn off. The rats gnawed away at their bars, Mrs. Allsopp wrote a sentence on the board and underlined it, and Karen Sharkey leaned behind Fran to whisper to her friend Alison. Fran yawned. Another twenty-five minutes till break.

". . . and turn to page one oh four and copy out the diagram. All right?" Mrs. Allsopp put down her chalk and disappeared next door into the chemistry lab where Mr. Downing was teaching. Everyone sat back and began to talk.

"Have you seen the way them two carry on? It's disgusting!" Karen Sharkey sucked on her pencil and looked around the table suggestively.

"Dirty cow," said Alison.

"Allsopp or Karen?" Fran asked quickly for a laugh.

"Both of them," Alison said indifferently. "He is nice though, Mr. Downing, isn't he? I like men with blond hair."

"He's all right," Karen conceded. "His breath frigging stinks, though. When he bends over your book and you get a whiff of it—" She slumped dramatically over in a dead faint.

"Quit it, will you?"

Alison did not appreciate being fainted over. She rammed her elbow into Karen's heavy side, and Karen retaliated with a shove. From across the room one or two of the boys whistled and clapped. Karen and Alison showed them two fingers at once, and dropped into a confidential chat about Karen's boyfriend, leaving Fran out of it. Bored, she began to turn the pages of the textbook as the noise level rose. The boys began to run around, opening the windows and leaning out, or crawling under the tables. Fran wished Allsopp would come back. She hated the disorder even more than the lesson. Flipping through the pages of the book, she remembered what Hilary had said last night, about waste. I wish they'd *make* us work, she thought. I wish I'd learned something here. But I don't suppose I could understand any of this, even if I tried.

On the next page there was a photograph of a bird in flight. Underneath were diagrams showing the action of the wings. Something about those clear lines arrested Fran.

"It's beautiful," she said out loud.

The other two looked at her and then at each other.

A GIFT FOR A GIFT

"Poor cow thinks she's a genius," Karen said.

That was the trouble they had with Fran. With a family like hers she was lucky they let her sit with them at all, really. And sometimes she smelled. But she was all right most of the time, only now and then she came out with something that got her in good with the teachers. As if she thought she was something special, as if the class wasn't good enough for her, and that's why she was absent, when everyone knew she had to stay at home to look after her mother who ought to be put away. But before they could remind her of all this, Mrs. Allsopp came back and began to yell. She had just gotten the boys sitting down when the bell went and they all shot up again.

"Those of you with books, I want that diagram finished for next time," she shrilled above the noise.

Fat chance, thought Fran. But she took the book all the same.

The others piled down the stairs, but Fran pushed her way up against the flow of the crowd. On the next floor she went over to the window and rested her elbows on the ledge until the last of the kids had drifted away. A teacher came out of a classroom with an armful of exercise books, shot a swift glance at Fran, but went on toward the stairs without ordering her outside. Fran stood at the window a little longer, enjoying the quiet; then she went over to the book closet.

It was a narrow room, just wide enough for a window at the far end. Fran often came here at break or dinnertime to read.

Though she never thought about it if she could help it, she supposed the teachers knew; they certainly never stopped her. Under the window was a radiator and in front of that a desk. Fran sat down on the desk and hugged the radiator, more for comfort than for warmth. She opened the biology book and found the diagrams of the bird in flight. She started to read the text. Through the dry scientific prose she caught a glimpse of the bird that had broken into her mind the evening before. She looked at the diagrams again and suddenly saw how they worked, grasped the sense of it, and through the sense the beauty. Excited, she got up and went to the shelves to look for a book she had read before, a small book with a dingy blue cover, a poetry anthology. She couldn't remember exactly what she was looking for, but she knew it was in that book. Then there it was. She had found it.

> *Thou wast not born for death, immortal Bird!*
> *No hungry generations tread thee down;*
> *The voice I hear this passing night was heard*
> *In ancient days by emperor and clown:*
> *Perhaps the self-same song that found a path*
> *Through the sad heart of Ruth, when, sick for home,*
> *She stood in tears amid the alien corn;*
> *The same that oft-times hath*
> *Charm'd magic casements, opening on the foam*
> *Of perilous seas, in faery lands forlorn.*

It was the same thing. The poem and the science were the same thing. A law and a beauty—her mind fell silent, struggling with something she could not grasp. When the bell rang, she let it go. She sat for a while, not wanting to leave the quiet, but eventually she got up and joined the crush in the corridor. It was only later, pushing into the classroom for her next lesson, that she realized she was close to tears. It was grief she was feeling, an almost unbearable sense of loss. But what had she lost?

She took a seat at the back by the window. Outside, some boys were playing soccer; their shouts came faintly through the glass. Fran wished she could be out there instead of in Mr. Headley's English class. Mr. Headley was trying to launch the class into a discussion about crime and society. Fran paid no heed. If I thought that really existed, she was telling herself, if that bird was something real—

"So without the police," Mr. Headley's voice boomed into her ears, "what would we be left with?"

"Some great laughs," called out one of the boys at the back.

"Such as?"

"You wouldn't have to worry about getting served in a pub. And you could steal whatever you liked. No one could stop you."

Mr. Headley whistled.

"And what if someone stole your stuff?"

"Easy." The boy grinned around at his pals. "I'd kick their heads in."

Mr. Headley raised his voice above the snickering and banter.

"So is there no one in this class who thinks the police is a good idea?" Some of the girls virtuously put their hands up.

Oh, Christ, thought Fran, and turned to look out of the window again.

When she turned back, Mr. Headley was standing in front of her desk. The class was giggling.

"You didn't hear the question, did you, Fran?" he said.

Fran looked at him sullenly. She didn't like Mr. Headley. He had a big funny-looking mustache that covered some kind of scar on his upper lip. The boys called him Groucho. He had no trouble keeping order and he was popular all right, but Fran hated the way he picked on people and made sarcastic little jokes about them for the rest of the class. And he was always trying to get her to join in things. She wished he would just leave her alone.

"Come on, Fran, wake up," he said. "Tell us what you think. Give us the benefit of your superior insight."

"About the police?"

"Oh, so you were listening. We did wonder."

Fran hated that "we." She paused as if thinking hard. Then her face cleared.

"Dunno," she said brightly. "Sorry."

Mr. Headley looked at her. Fran looked straight back. There was a silence.

"I see," said Mr. Headley.

Fran shrugged, and grinned a little. She thought she had won. But Mr. Headley hadn't finished. His eyes above the big mustache were angry and when he spoke his voice was brittle with irritation.

"You think that's enough, do you, Fran? You think it's all right to sit at the back with that bored look on your face? That's when you can be bothered to come in at all, of course."

Fran unfolded her arms, bit her nails, and looked away.

"Sometimes I think you're just stupid," he continued. "You act like you're stupid. But it's only an act, Fran, isn't it? I know what you're capable of reading when you think there's no one around to see you. But you won't share it, will you, Fran? You won't let anyone else have the benefit of your brains. You'd rather just sit there feeling superior, right?"

Fran stared down at the desk, slowly turning red. She could feel the class around her like a pack, stirring with excitement. They were loving it.

"So open your mouth, Fran," said Mr. Headley. "Show us what we've been missing."

Fran stared past him at the wall. She swallowed hard. "About the police?"

"That's right. About the police and the law."

"All right," Fran said quickly. "I think the police make not a goddamn difference and I think the law makes not a goddamn difference."

"Fran—" Mr. Headley said warningly.

"I mean it!" She looked at him in quick appeal. "They don't change anything, do they? They can't. They can only stop you from doing things. They can't stop you from thinking. They can't change what's there." She paused. It had been a balance, a unity. She had almost approached it . . .

"The law's only right and wrong," she said. "Good and evil's what's real."

"I don't see the difference," said Mr. Headley. "What's the difference?" Fran couldn't explain. She didn't understand it herself. She was struggling in the dark, groping for what she had seen.

"It's . . ." She stopped, and gave up.

Someone across the room snickered. "What's she talking about, sir?"

"She's only showing off. Thinks she's pretty clever, Fran Kelly."

Mr. Headley smiled. "I must admit—" he began lightly.

That was enough for Fran. She was on her feet, stung deep in her pride.

"Goddamn you, then," she said. "You were the one that told me I had to say."

"Fran—"

She paid him no heed. She looked around at the delighted class. "Goddamn all of you," she said, and walked out.

"That," said Michael at the school gate, "was rather a silly outburst, if you don't mind me saying so."

"I do mind," Fran retorted angrily. She was not at all pleased to see him. "What are you doing here, anyway?"

"I came to meet you. Come on." He took her arm.

Fran resisted. "Come on where?"

"Up onto the roof."

A GIFT FOR A GIFT

"The roof?" Fran stared. "What do you want to get out onto the roof for?"

"I like high places," said Michael simply.

He led her back into the school. There was no one in the entrance hall. As they passed the offices, they could hear the noise of typing from the secretaries' room and the bullying voice of the assistant principal on the phone.

"Up here," said Michael.

They began to climb the stairs that led to the domestic-science area. It was part of a three-story addition built onto the main body of the school. When they reached the second landing, Michael went over to the window and opened it.

"Look," he said. "It's easy. I'm surprised you've never done it." Just below the window was the roof of the main building. They climbed out onto it. It was flat and dry, with a low parapet at the edge. It would be a good place for a game of soccer, Fran thought, provided you had strong nerves. Michael walked to the edge and looked down.

"Someone will see us," Fran said.

"No, they won't."

Under Fran's feet were classrooms where lessons were going on. She could almost feel the atmosphere in each, the warm din of the last lesson of the day. It gave her a queer feeling to be walking over them. She looked up into the classrooms of the domestic-science area. Girls and boys moved about, absorbed in different projects. Not one of them lifted their eyes to the window. And she was walking on the roof with the wind in her face! She stretched her arms and wanted to shout.

"Fran, come here."

She had almost forgotten Michael. She went to him with some reluctance. There was a quietness in his pose at the roof's edge, and a lack of expression in his face as she walked toward him that made her uneasy. When she reached him, he said: "I gather you and Hilary have been conspiring against me."

His tone was light, his manner smooth and cold. It was impossible to tell if he was angry or joking.

"I don't know what you mean," Fran said uneasily.

"Don't you? The two of you were very confidential last night after midnight. All my shortcomings discussed at length."

Fran looked away. "Sorry," she muttered.

"The worst of it is, you've upset Hilary."

Fran turned to him quickly. "Upset Hilary? How?"

"Oh, I don't mean she's angry with *you*." The ghost of a grin crossed Michael's face. "It's me she's turned against. She won't be able to keep it up, of course, but for the moment I can't get into the house. I'm banished."

"Why?" Fran felt a little less concerned now she knew it was Michael's problem. "What have you done?"

"Oh, it's nothing I've done. Even Hilary isn't ungrateful enough to try and pretend it's that. But I can't get it out of her exactly. All she'll say is that she has something she needs to straighten out with you." He grinned. "Actually, I know what it is. But I won't spoil it for you. She wants you to go and see her."

"What, now?"

"Oh, I think it'll keep for a while. In the meantime," he looked at her sideways, "I think we should try and find something to take your mind off Mr. Headley and the unattainable good."

Before Fran could ask him what he meant, the school bell rang. Under their feet there was a subdued roar as chairs were scraped back and classrooms began to empty. Michael took Fran's hand.

"Quickly," he said. "Before they all come out."

They began to rise into the air very gently. The movement was so sudden that Fran only noticed when her stomach began to be sucked empty, as if she were going up in an elevator. When she looked down there were two yards of nothing between her and the roof. She lurched toward Michael, grabbing at him with both hands.

"You're safe," he said. "I won't let you go."

Suddenly the world turned sideways. They began to move like swimmers through the air. Fran spread out her free hand and felt the wind rushing through her fingers. Down below them the school was shrinking; the roof was as small as a rug. Fran squeezed Michael's hand.

"How did you know I always wanted to—"

But the wind, battering at her mouth, tore the words away.

●

MAEVE HENRY

They were gathering speed and height. Fran could see the road beside the school field below them, and the houses all around the school. The parked cars were as small as buttons. The wind was in her hair and her clothes; her shirt fluttered like a sail and she gasped with cold. The wind pressed on her lungs like a board. She was a stiff kite, riding the currents at Michael's side.

The whole town was below them now, a red and brown and gray confusion, slipping southward. They were following the road that led north to the sea, past the abandoned steel mills and the little railroad line. Fran could now see the long curve of the coast, from the gleaming white power station to the yellow cliffs at Sandiwell. They reached the outskirts of Coatham, the local seaside town, and began to lose height rapidly. Fran's arms were aching and her neck was stiff with the effort of keeping her head up against the wind. They passed trailers and the amusement park, the dunes and the wide beach, and now the sea was under them, glassy green in the afternoon sun. They dropped like birds, skimming the sharp tips of the waves. In her exhilaration, Fran let go of Michael's hand. For a moment she was terrified, then she soared upward and twisted in the air. She could fly without Michael! As she dived again, spray dashed into her face. She laughed and scooped up a handful of sea water and flung it at Michael. He let out a yell and began to chase her. Fran screamed in mock terror and struggled to get away, but he was faster and more powerful than she was. He caught her by the shoulders and twisted her around to face him.

A GIFT FOR A GIFT

"I'm good to you, aren't I?" he said.

When she did not reply he gave her shoulders a little shake. "Aren't I?" he insisted.

She looked at him and nodded slowly. Suddenly she was afraid. "You'll go away," she said in a small voice. "Like my dad."

"I'll take you with me."

Fran only looked at him.

"I'll take you with me," he repeated. "All your wishes, Fran, I promise." He leaned forward and kissed her on the mouth. Then he pushed her gently down. Fran found her feet resting on something hard. The green of the sea had hardened into the green of the school field.

Fran pressed the back of her hand to her mouth.

"You," she said.

CHAPTER EIGHT

They sat on the wall outside the school for a short time after that. Fran did not want Michael to go. She kicked her heels gently against the bricks and looked sideways at him. He touched her hand and said: "Don't forget Hilary wants to see you."

"And where will you be, if you can't come to the house?"

"Never you mind. You don't have to know everything, do you?"

" 'Course not," Fran said insincerely.

"And it won't be very long before Hilary's too weak to keep me out," he continued. "It's already cost her quite an effort. And then . . ."

Fran suddenly felt cold. She slipped down from the wall and stood in the street, staring at the houses opposite.

"What's the matter, Fran?"

"Nothing."

"Tell me."

A GIFT FOR A GIFT

He came up behind her. Fran said quickly: "Hilary told me what you made her promise, that's all."

Michael sighed. He was so close Fran felt his breath on her neck. A moment later she turned around and found the street empty.

Slowly she began to walk in the direction of Hilary's. But she didn't want to see the old woman just yet. She was too troubled, too confused. Instead, she found herself heading home.

When she got there and saw the state of the place, she bitterly regretted having come. All the plates in the kitchen were somehow dirty again. There was a sticky brown mess trodden into the linoleum and the broken flap of the kitchen table had finally come off its hinges. Neither of the boys appeared to be home, which was lucky for them. Fran picked up a pair of dirty underpants and a towel from the hallway and headed upstairs. She could not face the living room.

Her mother's bedroom door was ajar. Fran could hear a radio playing country and western, and her mother singing along in a loud untuneful voice. When she looked in she saw her mother sitting on the bed, painting her toenails pink.

"Mom?"

Her mother's hand jerked in surprise. She glanced around and then back. "Now you've made me smudge it," she complained.

She finished the last toe and extended her foot for Fran to

see. "Do you like the color? I thought it'd cheer me up a little."

Fran looked at her mother's feet. They were attractive, plump, and pretty. A kind of unease made her snicker. She said: "Who's going to look at your feet when they've seen the rest of you?" Her mother's mouth slopped open. For a moment she just stared at Fran. Then she said in a voice so small and hurt it was like a child's: "All I wish is that some-day, someday, you'll have a daughter that'll speak to you the way you speak to me. Then you'll know what it's like—" She broke into heavy tears, her body shaking like a blanc-mange under her pink nightie.

"Oh, *Mom*—"

Fran was embarrassed and distressed. It cost an effort to touch her mother, but she put a hand on her shoulder.

"If you knew how bad I feel," her mother sobbed.

"I do know." Fran stroked her arm. "I do know, Mom."

"No, you don't." She turned away, wiping her eyes and sniffing violently. "If you did, you wouldn't be so nasty to me. You think I'm like this on purpose. You think I don't care about you and the boys."

Fran's hand stopped moving. "If you care," she said in a tight voice, "why don't you do something?"

Fresh tears welled from her mother's eyes. "What can I do? It's gotten to be too much for me."

Fran sat down on the bed beside her. She remembered Michael's promise and his powers. "Mom," she said with an awkward laugh. "What if I won the lottery or something like that? Would that help?"

Her mother hunched herself together, elbows on thighs. "You never would."

Her eyes grew brighter all the same. She loved a daydream.

"Pretend," said Fran. "Pretend I have. What would you do with a million, Mom? You could have your own house, a really posh one."

"And someone in every day to clean it."

"And you'd never have to cook. You could eat Chinese take-out every night."

"I'd pay everything off, and get the boys some nice clothes. Lee could go on that soccer-coaching vacation he's been talking about."

"Lee could go wherever he likes. The farther the better."

"Fran, honestly!" But she was giggling, she felt better.

"You could have whatever you like," said Fran, warm with her own generosity. "You could burn this dump down and start again. Because you see, Mom—"

But before she could begin her explanation, noise erupted downstairs. "Christ, that's them back," said her mother. "There's nothing for them to eat, either." She looked at Fran. "How are things at this new place of yours, then? You're not back because of any trouble?"

"No, Mom."

"I do worry about you, you know."

"Yeah?" Fran's voice was carefully indifferent. "Listen, Mom, about the money—"

But her mother hadn't finished. "I knew you'd want to

move out sooner or later," she said. "Well, you haven't much to stay for, have you? This place. The boys. I'm not blaming you, Fran. You missed all your chances with me, I know that."

"No worse for me than for the boys," said Fran, stiff with embarrassment.

"No, except you were the clever one," her mother said. "I know how much you like books. If I'd known what books to buy you, love, if we'd ever had any money—"

"I didn't think you'd noticed," Fran said dully. She was shaken. She thought of all the cosmetics cases and board games and awful crocheted sweaters Christmas and her birthday had produced. How could love be so feeble? Hadn't her mother heard of goddamn book gift certificates? Couldn't she have asked?

"And all those different schools you went to when you were in and out of public assistance," her mother was saying. "It can't have been easy for you. But I think you could still do it, Fran. If you wanted. I've been thinking, you see. You could stay on and study for some exams. If it's quiet and they're nice, maybe you could do it where you're living now. Or perhaps you could stay with your gran down in Bournemouth. She'd be glad to do something for one of you. I've kept her out of things a little. I've always felt bad about not making a go of things, not like your auntie Di. I've always been the stupid one in the family. Fat and stupid, that's me." She gave a nervous little laugh and looked at Fran. "And I'll manage with the boys. I'll have to, won't I?"

Fran said nothing. She could not trust herself to speak.

A GIFT FOR A GIFT

•

Her mother clambered back into bed.

"Just listen to them downstairs," she said. "You couldn't do something about their tea before you go, could you, Fran?"

"Yeah, all right." She moved toward the door, then turned to face her mother. "If I did stay on," she said, "it'd have to be somewhere else. I'm not going back to that school. Not after Headley's lesson today."

"That's up to you, love."

"And would you really be able to manage? If you had a little more money or something?"

Her mother smiled. "I don't know where you think it's going to come from," she said. "But you worry about yourself. We'll be all right."

As Fran went slowly downstairs the yelling and screaming from the living room got louder. When she opened the door, she saw Lee sitting on top of Nigel, banging him in the chest with the wastepaper basket. Every time he hit him more paper and ash and scraps of food fell out. Nigel had his eyes closed; he was screaming on one continuous note that became a gurgle whenever Lee struck him. Lee was chanting: "You goddamn *will,* you goddamn *will,* you goddamn *will*—"

Neither of them seemed particularly upset, but Fran just couldn't stand it. She shouted: "Get off him, Lee!"

Lee was making too much noise to hear her.

"Get off him!" She crossed the room and grabbed his shirt collar. Lee flailed out with an arm, dislodging her grip. "Piss off, Fran!"

So Fran got hold of him by his hair. That was Lee's weak spot; his scalp was incredibly sensitive. She pulled hard and went on pulling. Lee dropped the wastebasket and began to scream. Slowly, keeping well out of range of his fists, Fran pulled him to his feet. As soon as the pressure was off his legs, Nigel scrambled away to safety behind the settee. Then Fran let go of Lee and jumped back. He turned, panting, tears of anger and pain in his eyes.

"Fran, you bastard!"

Fran dodged farther away, afraid he was going to hit her. Instead he jerked his head toward Nigel, transfixed already by the cartoon on TV. "Look, the little bastard's not even crying. Anyway, it was his fault."

"Oh, yeah?"

"Yeah. I told him to take out the wastebasket and he wouldn't."

Fran was filled with an overwhelming tiredness. She looked around the room.

"Look at the mess, Lee," she said. "Just look at it. And you made a fuss about him taking out the wastebasket?"

He lowered his head bullishly. "I'm just trying to make him behave. You're too soft on him, Fran. It's not good for him. Someone's got to try and toughen him up."

"God, you make me sick," she said. She called over to Nigel.

"Are you all right, Nige?"

"What?"

He wasn't listening. The bright chatter of the cartoon filled his world.

A GIFT FOR A GIFT

•

Fran's resentment deepened. With a bad grace she went over and started picking up some of the mess. To her surprise, Lee gave her a hand. "Fran," he began. His voice was unusually hesitant.

"Oh, what is it now?" she snapped.

"Are you really not coming back?"

She straightened up and looked at him. He was scowling down at the carpet, nudging an empty tin can with his foot.

"Why?" she asked in a hard voice.

Still not looking at her, he said: "Because it's worse when you're not here."

That was a lot, coming from Lee. But it was still only words. Fran's resentment was not assuaged. "If you'd ever given me a hand when I was here," she began. Lee did not stop to hear the rest of it. He hunched his shoulders and made for the door.

"I don't know, all right?" Fran yelled after him. "I just don't know." The slam of the front door was his reply.

As soon as he had gone, Nigel started whining.

"All right, sunshine," said Fran wearily. "Let's get you cleaned up, shall we? You're covered in muck from that wastebasket."

She carted him upstairs, half carrying him, half dragging him like a much younger child. In the bathroom she was tempted to slap him, he got on her nerves so much.

"What's the matter with you?" she demanded. "You were all right till a minute ago."

"You said you weren't going away again, you said."

Fran had been expecting that. She still didn't like it when it came. "Yeah, well. People don't always do what they say," she told him callously. She took the washcloth and attacked his face with it. But as soon as he could twist his mouth free he was at it again.

"When are you coming home, Franny?"

"I don't know, I don't know, I don't know! Jesus, I never should have come by today. And don't wail . . ." She raised a warning hand. "I'm not in the mood for trouble, understand?"

Nigel collapsed limply against her again. "I want you home," he whispered.

Fran felt terrible. She ruffled his hair.

"I know," she said.

She set him on his feet and gave him the towel. She pulled the plug out of the basin and watched the water go. Could Mom really manage on her own? It was rubbish to think that money would make any difference to the way Lee was. And it was her Nigel wanted, not some paid baby-sitter. But I want my own life, Fran thought. I want Michael.

"I saw Dad yesterday," Nigel mumbled indistinctly from inside the folds of the towel.

"What?"

"Dad. I saw him yesterday outside the OTB."

"I'm surprised you recognized him," Fran said sardonically. But the thought of her father cheered her up as it always did, and it gave her a new idea.

A GIFT FOR A GIFT

•

She took Nigel down to the kitchen, found a can of tomato soup and the bread and gave him his tea. She let him take it into the living room and once he was settled in front of the television said firmly: "I'm going now, Nigel, all right?"

"Yeah."

He didn't turn his head. But as she opened the door she heard him starting to cry. For a long moment she stood with her hand on the door, then shut it on him quietly. Nigel would be all right. She had her plan.

Her father was sitting on Mrs. Thomas's gold dralon sofa, watching the news on television. He sat forward, his small hands wedged between his thighs and his head raised a little, completely absorbed. Fran watched him through the picture window, standing on the gravel by the big tub of plants. When she rapped on the glass he turned, stared, and got up, unsmiling, to let her in.

"Hello, Fran love, nice to see you," he said.

"Hello, Dad. You're looking well."

He was. In his neatly pressed jeans and shirt he looked like the father in a cornflakes commercial. But the way he was standing, leaning with his arm against the wall, meant that Fran could only just step inside the door.

"And how's your Mom?"

"Not so good," Fran said. "That's one of the reasons I came by to see you."

"If the other's what I think it is, then you're out of luck," he said with a laugh. "I lost a bundle on the horses yesterday."

"It's not money, Dad. It's the boys."

Her father sighed and dropped his arm like a householder worn down by a salesman.

"Come on in, then."

Fran followed him into the living room. She never liked to sit down in it. The big armchairs that matched the sofa were still wrapped in the original plastic, to keep them clean. Fran sat down on the edge of one of them, opposite the display unit that housed Mrs. Thomas's collection of glass novelties. Her father stood, one hand on the television. He had turned the sound down, but he went on watching the pictures, his lips moving slightly as if he were trying to learn to lip-read.

"I said it was about the boys."

"Oh, yes." Reluctantly he turned around. He was such an attractive man, so capable-looking, that Fran simply blurted out to him: "Dad, couldn't you have them to live here?"

She knew before she'd finished saying it that it was a mistake, that she should have led up to it. But she went on quickly. "I don't mean forever. I just mean till Mom gets back on her feet. Lee's such a handful now. He really needs a man to straighten him out, he's beyond Mom anyhow. And Nigel needs someone who can keep a proper eye on him. I'm not living at home now—"

"You're not?"

"No. And you know how Mom gets. She can't cope with anything at the moment. It's Nigel I'm really worried about.

A GIFT FOR A GIFT

He'll end up worse than Lee if nobody does anything—always assuming Lee doesn't kill him first."

Her father said nothing. He just stood looking at her with a faint smile on his face. She had seen that smile so often when he had been living at home. He wore it when Mom and he were arguing about money. It was one of the things she had always hated in her mother, the way she nagged Dad. But now she remembered something else. Her dad had smiled, but it was always Mom who went down to the welfare office. It was always Mom who had done the hard things.

"Think of my situation, love," he said now. "It isn't my house, you know."

"You could ask her," Fran said.

He grinned and looked at her ruefully, eyes round and blue as Nigel's. He had such a winning face.

"You wouldn't want to get me into a fight, would you?" he said.

In all the fights, in all the trouble at home, Fran remembered, he had never lost his temper. And he had never done a thing that didn't suit him. For a moment she thought of making him do it, of using Michael's power to force it to happen. But her anger didn't last. His charm saved him, as it always had.

"It's all right, Dad," she said. "I'll think of something else."

He had the grace to look sheepish.

"Irene'd say no anyway."

"It's all right, I've told you. No need for excuses."

He opened his mouth, thought better of it, and sat down near her.

"And how are you, pet?" he said comfortably. "You've moved out, you said. Boyfriend, is it?"

"No."

"Friends, then. Amazing. It doesn't seem all that long ago that you were just a little thing. Do you remember that game we used to play, looking at things in the stores?"

"Yes, Dad."

She wanted him to stop and not spoil it. She wanted to remember it herself, not hear it from him in a voice grown sugary with sentiment. "Funny, the things you remember. I promised you a pair of ice skates once. They were in the window of the sporting-goods store. You were crazy about them."

"I don't remember," Fran said bleakly.

"Don't you? It was just after your Mom went to the hospital for the second or third time, and I came here."

"When you left her, you mean, and we had to go on public assistance again?"

If he noticed the edge to her voice he didn't react to it. "Yes, that's right. You wanted those skates so badly. You were going to be a champion, you said."

"But there isn't a rink," said Fran. "Not for miles."

She couldn't recognize herself in the story at all.

"You really don't remember?" He looked at her and laughed. "And that's the one thing I've always felt bad about, not getting you those skates."

"The one thing?"

She looked at him with open hostility.

"Come on, love," he said. "I'm only human. Your mom doesn't bear a grudge."

"That's nice of her," said Fran. "And nice for you and Irene."

She got up to go. She looked around the room where everything was so neat and comfortable, then down at her dad's feet in their clean brown socks. Had she ever wanted to be a skater? If so, it had been one of those brief dreams that leave no scars or memories. He doesn't know me, she thought. Not really. Not like Mom.

"Well . . ." she said.

"You're going, are you, love?" His face brightened. "I'll see you out."

At the door he put his hand on her arm.

"Don't leave it so long next time, all right?"

"Sure, Dad."

"Give my love to the boys."

"Sure."

As she walked away, Fran looked back once at the neat little house with its tubs of plants and its crazy paving. Imagine Lee and Nigel there, she thought with scorn. Imagine anything that real.

CHAPTER NINE

BEFORE GOING BACK TO Hilary's, Fran went home again. She got in the back way without disturbing Nigel and left a note on the kitchen table for her mother, giving Hilary's address. She wasn't sure why she did it. Just in case, she told herself.

When she reached Hilary's, it was getting dark. The bedroom smelled close and sour. Fran drew the curtains without waking the old woman, who was lying with her face turned sideways against the pillow, breathing rather heavily. Fran did not like to leave her, she looked so ill. She wondered if perhaps she ought to call an ambulance, but in the end she decided to wait. She sat down in the chair beside the bed and had a look at the pile of paperbacks on the bedside table. As she put one back rather clumsily, the whole pile tipped over and fell, and the noise woke Hilary.

"Fran?"

"Yes. Sorry."

"No, I'm glad you woke me. Did Michael tell you? I want to talk to you."

"He told me. He said you'd sent him away."

Hilary struggled to raise herself into a sitting position, failed, and flopped back with a weak laugh.

"Can you give me a hand? I'm almost done for."

Fran did her best. Her first couple of attempts failed because she was afraid of hurting the sick woman and so did not use her full strength. But at last she had her hauled upright and propped with cushions and pillows like a giant rag doll.

The effort had exhausted them both.

"Now," gasped Hilary. "About Michael. I'm keeping him out. That's one of the reasons why I'm in such a state. I'm battling against his will and the habits of a lifetime. But I have to do it, Fran, if I've any hope of making it permanent."

"Making it permanent?"

"Of keeping him out for good. Of leaving him behind me when I die." Fran's unease must have shown, for Hilary said impatiently: "Good God, girl, if I'm not afraid to talk about it, why should you be? It could happen anytime now."

That hardly helped to put Fran at her ease.

"Shouldn't we get you to a hospital?" she suggested unhappily.

Hilary's eyes blazed.

"Certainly not. I was born in this house and I have every right to die in it. What's the matter with you, Fran? Do you want to tidy me away like some unpleasantness?"

"No, but—"

"Well, then." She began to speak slowly, with many

pauses. "I want to die here, and I want to die without Michael. It's breaking a promise, I know, but the promise was unfair. I don't belong to him. None of us do. He's waiting for me to get weaker, waiting till I can no longer keep him out. When I haven't the strength to resist him I'll be his again unless—" She stopped and looked at Fran.

"Unless?" Fran repeated with a sinking heart.

"Unless you help me. I've been thinking, you see, about our strange overlap. It's like a gift, Fran. It's given me hope. I want you to help me to keep Michael out. Oh, I'm not asking you to give him up," she added savagely. "Just hold him off when I get too weak to do it, and afterward"—again she paused—"afterward you can have him to yourself."

Fran said nothing. She was torn between the desire to help Hilary and the fear that she might make Michael so angry he would abandon her. "I don't know if I can," she said at last.

"But will you try? Please, Fran."

Reluctantly, Fran nodded. After a moment she burst out: "What I don't understand is how Michael appears so terrible to you. When I'm with him—"

"I know," said Hilary in a dry whisper. "He's the possessor of great charm. But to be possessed by him—let's say I don't look forward to it. An intimate and infinitely prolonged encounter with emptiness. He's so very busy, Fran. But it's only a trick, a game he's playing with himself. Underneath he knows. He's simply out of place, refusing to move on."

"You've said that before," Fran told her rather resentfully. "But where should he be, if not here?"

Hilary sighed. "I know what I was taught in my childhood. Probably it's wrong to speculate about another's state. But I should say that Michael has refused to make the journey after death—the journey I want to make if I can get free of him." Suddenly she smiled. "He's such a child. A sulky child, standing on his mother's doorstep, too stubborn to go in."

Fran was not persuaded. "Go in where, though? Are you talking about heaven and God, stuff like that? I don't believe in stuff like that."

Hilary started to laugh. It turned into a cough that prevented her from speaking, and seemed almost likely to choke her. Fran attempted to rub her back, but Hilary waved her away. When at last it was over, she pulled at the pillows fretfully.

"I want to sleep," she said.

So Fran eased her down and switched off the light and sat down again to wait. It was quite dark now. The only sound was of Hilary's breathing, which grew noisier and less regular. Sometimes she began to draw breath, then stopped; there was silence until with a snort and a shudder her lungs resumed their action. Those moments were terrible for Fran. She dug her nails into her palms and could not breathe herself until the noise resumed. But as time passed she grew calmer, no longer afraid of what was coming. It was like arriving at the edge of the world. In a little while Michael would return and Fran would have to choose what to do. All her wishes, he had said. So much power, she thought, and I don't know what to do with it. To change things for me and the boys, I'd have to change Mom and Dad. I'd have to go back before we were even born. To change Mom and Dad I'd have to change their parents too. The chain goes back so far. I'd have to go right back to Adam and Eve, if there ever was an Adam and Eve. Can Michael's power go back that far?

A picture came to her of a red-haired Adam, standing in front of a closed door. It was just an ordinary house door, painted brown. Adam had the scared look of a child whose naughtiness had gotten out of hand. He had been crying. The dark girl beside him was tugging at his hand, trying to make him leave the door, but he wouldn't. Then, without warning or explanation, Michael was there. He pulled a key out of his pocket and held it out to Adam. Adam's face lit up; Fran could hear him singing as he fitted the key to the lock. Eve let go of his hand and tried out a step or two that might have been the beginning of a dance. But when the door swung open there wasn't a garden. There was only a crooked tree without leaves, a skull, and the smell of death.

It was horrible. Fran turned her head away and shut her eyes. When she opened them again the smell of death was still in the room. It was stronger if anything. It seemed to stand in the folds of the curtains and to lie along the bed. Fran brought her hands to her mouth and nearly gagged; her own skin stank of it. Then she realized what it was. The smell of death was the ordinary smell of everything, so familiar that Fran had to come to the edge of the world to notice it.

●

She sat for a long time without moving. None of Michael's wishes was stronger than the smell of death. That was what Hilary had tried to explain. That was why Hilary wanted to get away. Fran stood up and called softly.

"Michael!"

The air in the corner of the room by the door seemed to gather and thicken. "Is that you?" Fran peered into it. "Stop playing tricks. I'm sick of them."

The air grew black and took the shape of a man.

"You're so impatient," said Michael's voice out of it. It sounded as though he was smiling.

"Let me see you properly," Fran said angrily. "That's horrible."

"You really don't like tricks, do you?"

He was there now, solid and cheerful in a formal black suit, like a prosperous funeral director.

"Hilary's nearly at the end," he said. "I was coming anyway, but I'm glad you called me. Did she tell you what she wanted?"

"Yes. I'll come to that." There was something she wanted to ask him first on her own account. She fixed her eyes on his face and said uncertainly: "Michael, can I come to you without making any wishes?"

He looked puzzled.

"What would be the point of that? We have to have a bargain."

"I don't see why."

Michael sighed and moved toward her.

"What's gotten into you?" he said. "It's Hilary's doing, I suppose."

"It is not," Fran retorted, backing away just a little. "It's just—oh, Michael can't you see? There's something wrong with wishes. There's something wrong with 'I want.' There's no end to it, that's the trouble. I could wear you out with wishes and still not be happy. Changing things doesn't change anything."

She knew she was explaining badly, but she lacked the courage to tell him about Adam and the smell of death. She willed him to understand, but he only looked at her quizzically and said: "I see. Changing things doesn't change anything. That makes a lot of sense."

Fran turned away from him and walked over to the window. She pushed back the curtain and stared out at the dawn, pressing her forehead against the cold pane. Then she spoke, as quietly as if she was talking to herself.

"If that bird really existed, I'd believe it might be possible for things to change. If it existed, it might be possible to break the chain."

"Never mind the daydream," Michael said rather brutally. "Tell me about Hilary."

Fran bunched up the curtain and released it.

"She wants you to let her go."

"Surprise, surprise. But a promise is a promise."

Fran turned around. She blurted out: "What do you want Hilary for? You've got me."

Michael's face lit up. Fran was afraid to let him speak. She hurried on: "Why not let her go, Michael? She doesn't want to be with you anymore. She really doesn't."

Michael frowned. "And where's she to go if I don't have her?"

"Wherever it is people do go," Fran said. "Heaven."

Michael laughed. "You don't believe in heaven. I know you don't."

"Don't I?" Fran wasn't going to admit it to him. "Hilary does, though. She's the one that's trying to get there."

"Right," said Michael, nodding. "Now we're getting to the point. Hilary wants to get there. Fine. But she never told you much about the kind of life she led, did she? I was there, Fran. I saw it. And I can tell you that heaven will burn her like a fire at first. She'd be much better off staying with me than trying to endure it. I'll look after her. I'll look after both of you."

"But that's not what she wants," Fran said.

She was beginning to get frightened. Michael was like a kid that won't let go of a toy. She turned and looked at Hilary, still sleeping in the bed. Michael would make a ghost of her, trailing her at his heels wherever he went. And me, she thought. What will I become? She was aware of the edge of the world again. Now she could see the cold darkness beyond it.

"That's where you come from, isn't it?" she said to Michael. "The gap between the worlds."

She could see nothing beyond it. She didn't think there

could be anything beyond it. But Michael had spoken as if heaven was real.

"Please," she said. "Please let her go, Michael. I don't want to have to—"

But he was looking at Hilary.

"I've been good to her," he said quietly. "She won't send me away now."

That made Fran angry.

"No," she said. "I have to frigging do it."

Michael looked more amused than alarmed.

"She did say that, then? You'll never do it."

"Oh, won't I? Want to bet?"

But she was afraid. She didn't know if she could.

Michael said: "If you send me away, you know I won't come back."

That was what Fran had been dreading.

"Choose, Fran."

"I don't want to choose," she said in a low voice.

She looked back at Hilary in the bed, brown frizzy hair just visible above the tired white face. She didn't want to make a choice. They were tearing her apart between the two of them.

"You weren't very good to her," she said. "Not really. You never gave her what she wanted."

"Everything she asked for she got. She passed her exams. She had her lovers."

"You never got her father to love her."

"She never asked me to do that. I knew she wanted it,

but she never asked. So that doesn't count, I'm afraid. Besides—"

He was interrupted by a curious rasping noise from across the room. Hilary had woken and was trying to speak. Fran and Michael both moved quickly, but Michael got to the bed first.

"Michael."

To Fran's surprise and resentment, Hilary moved her hand to rest on his.

"It won't do, you know." She spoke in a slow and painfully weak voice. "Is Fran there? I can't see."

"I'm here," Fran said. She leaned past Michael and touched her on the arm.

"It won't do," Hilary murmured again. Her milky blue eyes stared past them. "It's too heavy to bear. And I've carried it with me for so long."

Fran turned to Michael.

"What's she talking about?" she whispered uneasily.

Michael shrugged.

Hilary's fingers fluttered over his hand.

"Michael?"

"I'm still here."

"Remember the beginning, Michael? Remember why I called to you?"

"Of course I do."

"Like a wound. All my life. To heal it, I have to be let go. Let me go, Michael."

Michael said nothing.

After a long pause, Hilary said: "Fran. You promised. To try."

She closed her eyes, and Michael laughed. It was the quiet laughter of pure amusement.

"It's a pity she never found that diary."

Fran glared at him, her eyes full of angry tears. "What diary? What are you talking about?"

"Her father kept a diary. I used to read it over his shoulder as he wrote it. I was going to tell you about it just now, before she woke up. He wrote pages about Hilary, how she tried too hard to please him, how she worked too hard at school. I suppose that's why he said all that nonsense about Classics that drove her half crazy. It was horribly clumsy, but he meant it for the best."

"You mean he did love her?"

"Of course he did. He just didn't know how to show it. There are a lot of people like that. When she won her scholarship to Oxford he went out into the back garden and cried, he was so proud of her."

Fran looked at Hilary. Her mouth had fallen open and there was a dribble of saliva on her chin. It was impossible to tell if she had heard. It was only then that Fran realized what Michael had done. "You never told her." She looked at him in disbelief. "You never told her!"

"She never asked me."

Fran felt quite sick. He was so pleased with himself.

"Don't you understand anything?" she said in despair.

Michael looked hurt. "It was a trick," he said. "If I'd told her, she wouldn't have needed me. It's like a joke, Fran. Can't you see the funny side?"

"The funny side!"

She wanted to beat the walls. But instead she bent down and gently wiped the saliva from Hilary's chin. There was a thin blue line around her lips and her skin felt clammy. Touching her, Fran felt her rage gather and focus, as if death was yet another of Michael's tricks. "All my wishes," she said savagely. "All right, Michael. What can I wish for that's stronger than death? What can I wish for that'll keep her from the cold and the dark?"

Somewhere in the silent room there came a noise, tiny at first, like the crackling of paper in a fire. Fran looked around, but she could see nothing. The noise grew quickly, filling the room with the roaring of an invisible fire. Michael called out: "Stop it, Fran!"

But Fran shouted: "It isn't me. I don't know what—"

She couldn't say any more. It was as if all the windows had blown open at once, filling the room with wind. The noise was extraordinary, and everything was stirring; Fran felt her hair blown back and saw the books ruffling open and the corners of the bedcovers lift. Then she raised her eyes and saw the cause. There was no roof to the house anymore. Above them was the early morning sky, and descending out of it a bird so beautiful that Fran cried out as if with pain. Tears filled her eyes as it approached. It was a dove, and its wings burned with light. It entered the room, flying so low and close Fran had to shut her eyes. As she opened them she saw it wheel and swoop over Hilary. One wing brushed Hilary's face, then it and she were gone and only Hilary's body remained.

There was a long silence during which Fran didn't want to speak. Then she said: "It exists."

Her voice seemed unnaturally loud in the stillness.

"It exists," Michael agreed.

Fran was shocked at how unhappy he sounded. She turned to him and was about to speak, but he said: "No, Fran, don't."

She took a step forward and to her distress Michael backed away.

"You let it in," he said. "You've made your choice."

Fran was close to tears.

"Can't I have both?"

He smiled.

"The raven and the dove? No, Fran."

"Then can't you—"

He shook his head.

"I'm not ready to touch the light. Not yet. Maybe not ever."

"Then what are we going to do?"

Before he could speak the doorbell rang, making Fran jump. She went to the window and looked out. A familiar small figure in a torn parka stood at the top of the steps.

"It's Nigel."

"You'd better see what he wants."

A GIFT FOR A GIFT

Fran half turned to him.

"I don't want—" she began, but Michael shook his head.

"Go, Fran."

She raced down the stairs and yanked open the front door.

"You've got to come," Nigel said at once. "Mom says you've got to come, Franny."

"Why? What's the matter?"

"Gran's here. She came on the overnight bus."

"What?"

"Lee phoned her yesterday. He asked her to come and straighten us out."

"Lee did?"

Fran couldn't believe it.

Nigel tugged her hand.

"Come *on,* Franny."

"Wait," she said. "Just wait here, all right? I'll be down, I promise." She slammed the door shut in his face and ran upstairs. But before she got to the top she knew. And when she entered the room, Michael was gone.

Fran walked over to the bed. She knelt down and touched Hilary's hand.

"He did love you," she said.

Then she got up and put on her coat. Thoughts of all kinds crowded into her mind. She'd have to tell someone that the old girl was dead. If Gran was going to stay, she could find out about a place to study at next year. And she would never, ever see Michael again.

●

She went through into the bedroom to collect her things. The bird existed, so somehow she would manage. Only she hadn't expected it to hurt as much as this. As she pressed down the lid of the suitcase she began to cry.

The doorbell rang again, raggedly at first, then long and loud.

"For God's sake," Fran yelled, straightening up. "I'm coming."

ABOUT THE AUTHOR

• • •

Maeve Henry lives and works in Oxford, England, where she writes and teaches English to foreign students. *A Gift for a Gift* is her second novel.